THE POLITICIAN
AND
PILLOW TALK

MEL FLAVELL

authormelflavell@gmail.com

ISBN NUMBER 978-0-9956302-1-5

Table of Contents

Characters in Order of Appearance

Captain Aaronovich	Capt. 'Ice Maiden'
Nicholas Baron (Nicholai Baronski) Russian Orphan	
Carole Semele	M15 Keeper of the pearls*
Stefan Baronski	Father of Nicholas
Peter Swayne	Friend of Carole Semele
Margaret Linley	Publican's daughter. Friend
Mr. & Mrs. Semele	Parents of Carole Semele
Sir Charles Willingham Wright	Head of MI5 section
Messrs. Jackson & Jackson	Letting Agents
Ian Duncan	Member of MI5
Georgiou Kadinsky	Acquaintance
Mr. & Mrs. Counter	Guardians to Nicholas
Alex Counter	Son of above
Past flat-mate to Carole	Member of MI5
Minister for War	
Russian Attache	
Mystery woman	Love triangle

*see The Prisoner and the Pearls Book 1

7

PART ONE

BASTILLE DAY FÊTE

PROLOGUE

The Finnish merchant ship slipped her moorings at the quayside and headed out for the Baltic Sea from Leningrad carrying an unusual cargo. They had been commissioned to take a cargo of horses. Fine animals from the Russian steppes near the River Volga, to assist their owner to bring a prisoner, a dissident author, out of Russia to western freedom, and had served them well as cover, on their trans-Siberian railway journey.

Another few minutes, and they would have been heading out to safer waters. But things had not gone to plan. As the very last minutes ticked by before their departure, a quarrel had erupted between the members of the family on the quayside. This incident had ended with his passenger receiving a slash wound to his cheek and uncle a chest wound.

They had managed the transfer of this beautiful cargo with the aid of the corn merchant who had brought their horses' requirements for the journey, and who was also due to sail on the 'Ice Maiden.'. As the Captain watched the quayside disappear behind him, he hoped that only medical services would arrive to attend the stricken man, lying on the quayside.

It was not unusual for the medical services to be needed on the docks. Sailors brawls often occurred when they had money in their pockets and taverns to spend it in.

Captain Aaronovich watched anxiously for the river police or customs officials for he did not want his ship to be inspected too closely, for one of his passengers was not on the manifest and his cargo, although perfectly legal, did not bear close inspection, for the animals were being attended by an irregular stable hand.

Slowly the ship made its way into open waters and the Captain called for a report on the condition of his 'bone fide' passenger, Nicholai Baronski, the owner of the cargo.

The Medical Officer, reported that they had stitched him 'real prettily,' because the bosun was used to these sewing jobs after his experience in trawlers. He reported that the invalid's cheek was an awful mangled mess and he had lost a lot of blood. The Bosun had stitched him up a treat and he was resting in sick bay like a baby. He shouldn't be troubling them for many hours, nor be able to help out with the horses. Calm them down, muck out, and feed them."

"Hm, that is unfortunate for I don't expect the crew to take on that job." Said Captain Aaronovich to the Medical Officer. "What about the corn merchant that first alerted us to the drama unfolding on the quayside. He's on board, I understand?"

"Yes Sir. He seems pretty handy, for he took charge of getting the parties on board and obtaining our medical assistance. I should say he must be handy around horses too, if he was bringing fodder, for the journey."

"Yes. Indeed." Captain Aaronovich said, for the less

they knew of his private arrangements, the better. For now, Nicholas Baronski, was safe and would heal as nature would let him.

The Captain pulled up his collar as he felt the icy chill in his veins. His knowledge of these waters brought back memories of another time and place. For the Captain was anxious to put as many sea miles as possible between his ship and the Russian sector of the Baltic Sea.

CHAPTER 1

Someone for Tea

The girl sat astern in the cockpit of the gently swaying boat as it lay anchored in Chelsea Harbour. She sat stroking a fat tabby cat that lay in her arms. It was a fat cat because it had been well fed and bore little resemblance to the scraggy cat of five months ago that had begged for food from her, one day in February.

She drank her tea and watched the sunrise over the River Thames, as it changed its colours from gold to orange and pink and purple and, as today, to grey, and she knew that the dawn's small promise of summer, had been withdrawn. Today it would rain. But for a few minutes more she was content to sit, eyes searching the skyline.

On the far bank, near to Chelsea Bridge, a man watched unobserved, as she sat with her drink. He had watched her every day for the past week and, every day, had done the same thing. Now it was Saturday and he had wondered whether there would be a change of routine, but there she was again.

Nicholas Baron was tired. Tired of the life that had set him roaming, and was glad to be back, glad to be home, glad to be near the one that he loved. But still Nicholas hesitated.

He had done all that was asked, and for which, was now nursing an injury. The result of a tragic narrow escape, too close for comfort, but he had recovered. At least nearly, for still he hesitated to take that final step. He did not wish to be pitied. Compassion, was not what he sought.

As the light strengthened, the watcher melted away to see to pressing duties.

He went to the early market in Battersea and turned towards the river once more, and to a small terraced house nearby. Inside a frail old man sat huddled in front of a fire with a thick blanket around and over his knees. The younger man closed the door and quickly went into the kitchen to brew some tea and put down the purchases on the table.

He went into the small parlour and knelt beside the sleeping man, adjusting the blankets around him and tucking his skeletal hands underneath, and watched the gentle breathing and was satisfied that the invalid still slept peacefully. Many nights had passed, while they had been together, when his sleep had been interrupted by wild screams from the invalid, and wondered at the images that his father was seeing, in these fitful dreams.

He sat in the chair opposite and found satisfaction in the transformation that he saw. Good nourishment and plenty of quiet rest were working a miracle in front of his eyes. His father Stefan, was getting stronger by the day, but the fire in his belly might take a lot longer to ignite.

When Nicholas had first seen his father, all the memories of childhood had been blown away with the shock at seeing his father's condition. A vibrant, laughing bear of a man, who had become a walking skeleton, with long matted hair and beard of such length that Methuselah sprang to mind, and the half-crazed look, was the only certainty, as he fixed his son with his moonlight blue eyes. Father and son stared, blue to blue.

Now his memory, thank God, had caught up with his recognition of that relationship and, piece-by-piece, Nicholas had been able to coax his father's mind to the future and the land they hoped to reach. Now, safe in this city of refugees and well-wishers, he was gradually gaining strength, and his son took pains to see to that progress.

The kettle began to sing and, as the man stirred, Nicholas turned back to the kitchen and poured the hot water onto Bovril and mixed it thoroughly. He cut chunks of bread, placed them on a blue and white striped plate and took them into the parlour, putting them next to his father's hand. He had been completely at a loss to know how to feed his father, as the harsh diet of so many years had made richer foods very hard to digest. He had found that a rotation of Bovril and bread, and bread and milk, occasionally with an egg in it, had been enough to raise the invalid's strength, but he longed to see him further recovered.

Today Nicholas had arranged for a doctor friend to check progress, and his landlady had promised to keep an eye on his father for a short while.

He had thought to go back to the river and perhaps continue his watch, from further down, where the willows along Battersea Park bent to the river. He cautiously turned his eyes northwest and looked across at Chelsea Harbour, seeing no sign of life on board, except the cat sitting on top of the cabin sunning herself.

After a few more minutes observation, he was convinced that the occupant was not in the boat. Against all resolve, Nicholas found himself over the bridge and heading for the motor cruiser. He did not wish to be seen but some compulsion brought him to this spot. He jumped from the gangway into the boat and from around his neck, took a key. Inside the cabin all was neat and tidy, and the array of female garments on the bed made him catch his breath, and close his eyes for one brief moment. He had seen the girl leave the boat on the Saturday, with a small suitcase and guessed that she would be away until today.

He put two logs on the fire and a kettle on the hob. He took two cups out of the cupboard and poured milk into them. When the tea was brewed, he poured it into one of the cups. With a sigh, he took up the one cup and drank from it, then lay on the bunk and gazed up at the bulkheads.

Memories of those precious moments before he had started on his journey, flooded in, and it was all he could do to return to the galley and out of the hatchway. He carefully locked the door and walked back up to the roadway, then, half walked and half ran, back across the river. He leaned exhausted against the balustrade, on the far side of the bridge. His returning strength was still very fragile.

The whole episode on the quayside of Leningrad had left Nicholas traumatised. No longer certain of anything, and the days that had followed in the sick bay had only delayed his complete understanding of family dynamics.

He had entered the adventure with high ideals and youthful enthusiasm and had not thought further of any consequences. He had then been able to think of his actions towards Carole more truthfully, when alone on the train to Geneva. The further family dynamics of his Uncle Dimitri and Aunt Babeta and their son Mikhail, of which he had learned in Leningrad, had been pushed to the back of his mind. It was too painful.

For they were his family, and he had automatically thought that they would be willing to help him − as indeed they had. Now he saw that he had not fully understood the undercurrent of animosity that had surfaced between himself and his cousin. Deeds that were done well before his own birth, had been revealed in those final few moments on the quayside. He had thought that he was entitled to the place in his father's life as his eldest son, until it had been revealed that his cousin Mikhail was actually his half-brother, 10 years his senior. This partly explained his animosity, as his aunt Babeta and step-father Dimitri had developed, a curious and distorted relationship with Mikhail and Nicholas.

The three men had travelled far into Siberia in their bid to rescue Stefan which had left them all physically drained and family tensions had erupted. In those final few minutes, there on the quayside, anger had flared and Mikhail had drawn a knife.

The whole truth of family relationships was revealed. In trying to placate Mikhail, he had swung the knife at Nicholas. His Uncle Dimitri had anticipated the action and, in deflecting the blade from Nicholas, had been stabbed in the chest.

Both severely wounded, it was left to a 'third party', Otto Strauss, to get Nicholas and his father onto the ship and to call an ambulance for the other stricken man. It was certain that his uncle had not died on the quayside, but any more information was not yet forthcoming, and Nicholas was left to make sense of his new-found knowledge.

His relationship with his father had been built on old memories and present compassion and he had not cared to examine it more closely. His own return to health had been difficult and the memory of the quayside quarrel had been buried for the time being.

CHAPTER 2

The Intruder

Carole Semele returned to the harbour as the sun was setting and was pleased to note that summer had returned. It had been a long and lonely winter and she had been glad of work to make her busy. Flat mate Janice, had been posted to Geneva and Carole's time in the flat had ended three months ago.

Some compulsion inside her had suggested, that she make use of the key that had been left for her by Nicholas with instructions to FEED THE CAT, the only acknowledgement that he would return. During the past four months, she had been living in the boat. It had been very cold and bleak on arrival, but once she had stoked the fire and checked the mechanics and bilges, to live there, had been the obvious thing to do.

No one had challenged her right of occupancy, as for days before, she had been coming to the river to feed the cat that pestered all the occupants.

This weekend she had taken a coach to Birmingham, and then another to Worcester, to stay with her parents, but their grief for her dead brother did not seem to be assuaged by her visit. That morning she had, briefly, seen

Peter Swayne at the Abbey, as he had finished his National Service and had applied to the Metropolitan River Police. He had been very interested in speaking to her, and especially enquired about her flat mate Janice. He had looked keenly at her, and seemed about to say something more, but was distracted by another person wanting to speak to him. Briefly he had given her his address and she had also given him directions to the boat.

The time had flown meeting old friends, and spending time on the river. She was feeling rather travel weary when she returned to the boat and opened the hatchway. Immediately she was aware of the welcoming warmth of the galley and saw the cups on the stove. She caught her breath, and a moment of fear transfixed her. Then remembering that her new training might be a nasty shock for any intruder, moved cautiously towards the far cabin and listened There was no sound and she sharply drew back the curtain.

Nothing! "Who's there?" She shouted at the heads, but there was no answer, and indeed no one was there either, or any indication of forced entry.

Carole sat on the bunk and reviewed the evidence, and something about the indicators of an intruder, set her heart racing. She looked in the stove and there two fresh logs burned brightly. She had not left the stove burning, that would have been far too dangerous, so someone had fed the burner. Was it for her? Who had set two mugs of tea on the side? She felt the kettle and touched the teapot and found warmth still in both. She drew breath and searched for any

Message, but found none. She scrambled onto the deck and searched upstream and down but by now the light was failing.

"Nicholas, oh Nicholas, can it be you." She whispered into the wind but nowhere could be seen any familiar figure.

Clouds scudded across the sky as the fine weather of the last week gave way to cold and damp, but still, every morning, she took her tea mug to the deck and watched dawn breaking. Most days, the sun did not appear, but she took comfort in the thought that he might be there.

For five days, she took her tea to the riverside and then trudged her way to Whitehall where she was being inducted into the world of the Foreign Office. She had often been away on weekend courses. There seemed an endless variety of events to continue her induction into the world of espionage and martial arts, and her days had passed swiftly enough.

She had suffered a broken heart, but her young spirit had recovered, and had entered into this new regime with enthusiasm and natural skill.

She was a strong swimmer and a natural around boats and water and had been promised a course of diving later in the summer. She had been enlisted into a local gymnasium and was now toning muscles with a workout, every day.

Her childhood playing, with her deceased brother, had

meant that vigorous roustabouts had been given full rein as she had been a tomboy when growing up. Each day that week it had rained but she donned her waterproofs and continued to drink her early morning tea watching for the return of the sun.

Nothing more had happened at the boat whilst at work, but on Friday evening, she had returned to a welcoming warmth and the kettle hot, with accompanying two cups laid out on the side. She sighed with relief and knew that this was a message.

Her weeks continued in this pattern, whatever the weather.

One weekend she had visited her home and her mother had lifted herself out of her lethargy sufficiently to bake a fruitcake for Carole and this she left out by the stove. When she returned in the evening the whole cake had disappeared. Carole agonized over where Nicholas could be. Surely, he was not on the streets, but why didn't he come to her as the exchange of gifts had established goodwill between them. What was stopping his return into her life?

****

The old man began to walk along the towpath with his son giving him his arm. Their progress was slow as they strolled in the sunshine. Spring had given way to summer and the old man took great pleasure in the warmth of the sun. Sometimes it became too much for him and they would return early to the little house.

Many hours were spent together exchanging news of their separate lives. It was very difficult for Nicholas to get any information from his father, but he could see that it gave him great pleasure to hear how Nicholas had lived, during their time apart.

It had been some weeks before he had told his father of his mother's death, but he seemed to be resigned to this. He supposed that his father had accepted their departure from his life, long ago, in order to endure the life that had been allotted to him.

It was a fine day and there were far more people along the towpath. They had strayed further than usual as his father had wanted to watch the activities on the river and enjoy the freedom of this random stroll. As they approached Chelsea Bridge, Nicholas saw a jogger coming towards him and his heart missed a beat. He recognised the colour of the tracksuit. He bent swiftly to adjust his footwear and averted his gaze, partially concealing his face behind his father.

It took all his willpower not to turn his gaze, when he saw Carole coming towards him, His duty to his father was still paramount and any chance of a future with her, would have to wait. As he drew abreast he turned his father away from the river, down a path, and disappeared behind a large hedge leading to the gates of the park. Behind him, he sensed a hesitancy in her stride but carried on walking until they were safely out of sight.

That evening, as they sat beside the electric fire, his father looked strangely at him. They had continued their walk home in silence and Nicholas had not broken it since, and there was a troubled look on his face.

"Son, I realise how much I owe to you for my rescue and know that this has been purchased at some cost, personally as well as financially. I have been so long having to think of my own survival that the instincts of civilization had quite left me. Now, by your care, I have recovered some of that cloak again."

"I propose that it will be better to restore my health if I go to live in the country for a while and let you pick up your old life."

"But Papa Stefan, how will you manage, you are still very weak?"

"Don't fret, if you would find a small Dacha, or cottage, in the country, and a housekeeper to see to my needs, I can enjoy this sunshine in the clean country air." He continued. "You know, of course, that I have not given up my writing and the country will be more suitable to the contemplation and reassessment of my work."

Nicholas looked at his father with concern in his eyes. "It is so soon, I don't think you should."

His father interrupted him with far more vigour than he had hitherto shown. "No, no, truly, if you can find me a place to stay, I can manage well enough. I might even let you come and visit me." He said, with an attempt at jocularity."

Nicholas looked at his father and knew that a landmark had been passed and he was on the road to recovery. He also had an idea where might be found, a suitable dwelling.

CHAPTER 3

The Estate Agent

As May passed into June, Carole was feeling confused about the mysterious comings and goings. She knew in her heart that it was Nicholas but she longed to see, and hold him, and give comfort for what might have been endured. She had only some idea that his flight had suited the British Government very well and that her part in that event had been pivotal. She had been told by Janice that the stolen pearls were to finance an escape plan for a dissident writer, Stefan Baronski. She had thought that a trap was being set for Nicholas, for MI5 and the newspaper article later had talked of an unknown male body washed up in the river. For many days, she had believed this to be Nicholas but had eventually learnt that it was not so. Then, the only hope that she had to hang on to, was the key to the boat. Now, she believed that he was back and was her mystery stoker. But why did he not reveal himself, when all she longed for was to hold him in her arms.

One day in June, she was just about to leave the boat for her usual jog along the embankment, when a middle-aged gentleman in a crumpled grey suit called. "Ahoy there anyone at home?"

She put her head out of the hatchway. "Who wants to know?"

"Ah, good morning young lady, I'm from Messrs. Jackson & Jackson, Letting Agents, Mr. Peter Stafford here at your service."

Carole was surprised at his obsequious manner as she had thought he was about to check her credentials.

"Come aboard, Mr. Stafford, would you like a cup of coffee?"

"No indeed, I won't interrupt you. I see you are about to go for a run. I just wanted to get some details about the rental."

"I understand that you are using the boat belonging to Mr. Nicholas Baron?"

"Yes, that is so." She said slowly.

"You do realise that the mooring will be up in a couple of months. Mr. Baron has asked me to ascertain whether you wish to continue the occupancy?"

"Of course," he went on officiously, "at this time of year the river boats are very popular for tenants and I could easily sub-let it for him elsewhere."

"Has Mr. Baron said he wishes me to leave?" She gulped.

"No, no, on the contrary, he was very particular about that. But he has to be out of town for a couple of weeks, on some family matter, and wanted to know whether you were happy to stay until his return, when perhaps other arrangements might be made. He has left it entirely to you to make your decision, but hopes you will enjoy the summer here and especially to 'feed the cat'." He joked.

Her heart skipped a beat and Mr. Stafford was treated to the most radiant of smiles from this charming young woman. Mr. Baron is a lucky man, he thought.

Carole took her morning run along the river and was hardly aware of her feet touching the ground. He had sent her a message. Something had prevented him from coming to her. 'Family matters'. Of course! She thought. Why didn't I think of that? He only had one family member, his father, and Nicholas had tried to get him out of the Gulag. Had he succeeded? She had forgotten, with all the mystery of the pearls, that they were to help refugees, and he would be one, wouldn't he?

Perhaps his presence here in West London must go unnoticed? There were plenty of people here in Chelsea who would recognise him and, indeed, who might wish him harm as, after all. Why had their friend Boris been murdered? She was convinced it was not accidental and the perpetrator might be on the lookout for Nicholas, should he ever return.

CHAPTER 4

The New Home - Intrigue

Nicholas drove his father to his new home, which had been chosen with care. His father had picked up his long unused English during the time of his recuperation. Nicholas had tried to speak to him in English to help him to fit into his new country and Stefan's command of the language had improved greatly but he was still anxious that his father would find things difficult independently, and he had taken the decision to stay with him for a little longer. He had sent a message to the Letting Agents and he hoped that Carole would understand what was being said.

Nicholas felt that his father still needed personal care. He had found Stefan a house near Carole's home in Worcestershire, hoping that his father would like the association with Shakespeare's country (at least the same river) and might result in a chance meeting with Carole or her parents. He couldn't bear the thought of leaving her behind in London. But his first duty was to his father's needs and he couldn't renege on that.

They arrived in Avonbridge as the Abbey struck the noon hour. They turned into the town square and Nicholas went into the Letting Agents to pick up the keys to the river cottage he had found. They turned towards the High Street and passed The Angel Inn.

A hundred yards up towards the Abbey was a small lane to the right, leading to the river and, twenty yards down, there was a large chestnut tree in the middle of a small green.

On the far side of this, stood a small cottage of red brick and pantiles. Two facing cottages made up the rest of the cul-de-sac. Around the tree was a seat made of wrought iron. To the right of the central house was a footpath that led down to the river. Further to the right, the Hotel gardens with chairs overlooking the orchard, led down to the river as well as linking it to a river walk.

Nicholas put the key into the oak and glass fronted door and entered a small square hallway with rooms leading off. Ahead, the door opened onto a wide sitting room with French windows leading out to the verandah. This was surrounded by trellis with rose bushes bowed down with their heady scented blooms, and beyond, a path led to a rough lawn, covered with dandelions and daisies, stretching down to the river.

"Nico, Nico, what a lovely home you have found me, how can I thank you." And Stefan's wrecked and wrinkled face was streaming with tears. "Here I shall truly find peace."

Nicholas gently turned his father back to the room and

gestured to the high-backed chair. "Stay here while I get all our things out of the car. I'll put the kettle on while you sit tight." Papa Stefan sank gratefully into the chair and marveled at how his life had taken such a wonderful turn.

Nicholas unloaded all the immediate necessities, made the tea to give to his father, and safely settled Stefan with a rug over his knees. Nicholas went up the High Street in search of some more substantial groceries and quickly found what he needed.

Next door was the Angel Hotel. He went inside and made enquiries about accommodation and was led to a large bedroom overlooking the garden and river beyond. He had thought it best to spend the first night here, whilst he aired and prepared the cottage for Papa Stefan.

He went down to the reception and enquired of the receptionist as to whether any nurse or local daily might be available. He explained his father's frailty and what would be required and the rosy cheeked young woman said she would give it some thought. He knew that here was the best place to start his search, as local extra help in the Inn was regularly needed, according to their seasonal requirements, and this bar maid would know much more about the casual labour available in the village. He had often found that they were a great source of information about locality.

Later, when he had tidied their belongings into the new house and taken the cases to The Angel, he had brought his father to sample the local fayre. Now his father was fast asleep and he had come down to the bar for a nightcap.

To his side was a table with several men sitting drinking. He had noticed them earlier, most especially the large gentleman with dark hair and the most extraordinary bushy handlebar moustache and plummy voice. They were laughing at something that had been said and he continued. "Yes, he is a bit of a dark horse, that new Minister for War. I don't know how he came to that position, he seems to have an eye for the ladies, I hear, and that is not a good recommendation for that job. He seems to mix with some very strange people; that Stephen Ward fellow is a bit creepy if you ask me." Nicholas strained to hear more but they had lowered their voices and moved closer to each other as an anecdote was exchanged, but a loud guffaw from all the group broke over him as they laughed knowingly at the comments made.

He had pricked up his ears at the mention of the name. He had been aware of the gentleman in question, when he had come to the reception last winter at the Russian Embassy, and he remembered his beautiful wife. Could that be a marriage of convenience? She was certainly an adornment to the life of a Minister. Social occasions meant that he needed a wife but it was well known that the life of an MP's wife was fraught with problems. Long sittings in the house and distance from their constituency, made married life hard to juggle, but that was what they signed up for, wasn't it? Here was a useful bit of information and he thought of a possible return to London to relate this to interested parties.

CHAPTER 5

The Kept Woman

Sir Charles Willingham Wright sat at his desk and looked at the painting before him and was very pleased with his purchase. It would be added to all his other curios in the glass case cabinet along the wall of his office.

It was a beautiful triptych of the 'Madonna of the Pearls of Sorrow' which added her tears to the pearls around her neck. The picture had a wooden gilded frame, with curious carving on it, which had proved to be Cyrillic writing. This had contained a message in code. In his profession, he came across such interesting pieces from time to time and enjoyed being reminded of the many ways that cryptology was used.

His latest purchase had come to him via a Finnish ship named 'Ice Maiden' and its captain had helped to solve a recent puzzle. It had aided the transfer of funds to friendly parties, to help British interests. He was about to further these once more. He had received disturbing news at the heart of Government, a possible leak of vital information to the Russian KGB, and he was about to put in place, a group of operatives who might be able to confirm or deny these rumours.

He very much feared that there had been a leak, but he needed proof if he was to take his knowledge to the Prime Minister. The level at which this might have occurred, was too serious to be ignored and must be stopped before any more damage could be done.

****

Carole had come back from Palace duty after the weekend of the Trooping of the Colour and was shocked to find an empty space, where once her home had been, and she blinked in disbelief.

Her eyes scoured the riverbank but nothing was to be seen. She had wondered whether another boat had anchored and shifted her boat along the pontoons but, no, there was nothing. Outside the pub opposite, sat the Letting Agent that had spoken to her before. At her arrival, he left his seat and headed towards the boat.

"Hello again, Miss. I suppose you are wondering where your boat has gone."

"Of course, I'm more than wondering. What the devil has happened to it?" As she felt a rising wave of panic and despair grip her.

"Don't be alarmed. I have been instructed to take the boat to the boatyard at Kingston. You know how this brackish water plays havoc with these vessels, and I understand that yours needs to be attended to."

How the, she stopped. What was the message this time? She waited for the young man to continue.

"I have been instructed to tell you that, in order not to inconvenience you whilst the re-fit is taking place, I am to give you this key to a flat in Dolphin Square. If you want any further information about this, I have here, the name of the boatyard upstream, at Kingston. In the meantime, you are at liberty to enjoy all the amenities of 'High Rise' living.

There are excellent facilities and there are several good restaurants in the vicinity. If you need some company whilst the owner is away." He added.

He smiled disarmingly at her, ending in a wink. He had decided to try his luck here, as it was obvious that her lover was far away; none the wiser if he were to share the man's courtesan, so to speak. He thought he would be sitting pretty in this situation as he had all the information and warning, of his return.

She looked at him with the full splendour of her smile and said sweetly. "That won't be necessary, thank you. I shall be far too busy to be in need of your company." Her smile turned to an expression of disdain that could freeze a sea-lion and he felt the force of her refusal, as if he were a worm crawling in some primordial mud.

When he was gone she looked down and stared at the key in her hand.

Is that what she was, some street life who had caught a rich 'sugar daddy' and was happy to play around on the side? Well the truth often got hidden in a lot of lies. She acknowledged to herself.

She recalled all the 'messages' that she had received so far this Spring and tried to find another explanation for them. She had longed to believe that it was Nicholas who had sent all the strange 'signs' in the galley of the boat, but was she a naïve fool who was being strung along (ouch) for other purposes.

She found a bench to sit on, her head now spinning in great confusion.

Nicholas, Nicholas, why do I care so much that it is you? Shall I only forever see you in the shadows around me? She anguished.

She looked up and saw the pleasure craft chugging up the river and thought that she might find further proof if she took a boat up the river. But was she stepping into a trap?

****

Sir Charles sat frowning at his desk. Usually very much in control of his world, the news he had just received, had disturbed him greatly. How could he explain the lack of vigilance?

Nicholas had been shown out of a side door onto the embankment just as Big Ben struck the 5 o'clock hour. He glanced up and his feet hesitated. It was only a short walk upstream to his boat, but no, he must see things through with his father and he was already late for his train. He turned away from the river bridge and right again, down the steps into Westminster Underground Station.

Two seconds later Carole hurrying to catch her train, turned left out of Whitehall and entered the same station. Two people on one escalator with dozens of commuters doing the same. At one point, Carole looked ahead of her and caught a glimpse of a man who reminded her of Nicholas and she focused more carefully. She laughed at herself, as she saw that this was a much older man and his profile was disfigured by a livid scar running along his jawline. A second later the man had reached the bottom of the escalator and turned left to the eastbound side of the line. This gave her more than a glimpse of his profile and the unmarked cheek that was turned towards her, made her catch her breath again. The certainty that it was Nicholas, came to her more forcefully. She followed his footsteps to the wrong side of the station but by the time she arrived, a train had just pulled away, leaving her distraught, on an empty platform.

Was it him? Had she imagined it? Her thoughts whirled about her head. Restoring a certain amount of calm to her fluttering heart, she instinctively knew, that the cat and mouse game he had played with her all summer, had been because of his changed appearance.

Once before she had seen a man coming towards her

that had made her stop, because he reminded her so much of Nicholas, but when she had turned around, he was gone. Had he been there all the time, but she had not the eyes to see behind the fresh scar that stared out of a face with eyes so blue.

****

Sir Charles poured himself a stiff whisky and splashed soda into the glass. His visitor was the second person to visit that afternoon and both had come with similar strands of information. After the satisfactory conclusion of the 'Madonna with the Tears of Pearls Affair', as he liked to think of it, he had been congratulating himself on keeping the lid on Anglo Russian affairs, but this newest information needed looking into.

His informers were linking the Minister of War with some very dubious characters and Sir Charles needed to know a lot more. If there had been a breach of security, between Britain and Russia, then security between the USA and Britain may also have been compromised. Khrushchev was certainly playing a dangerous game with his vocal support of Castro in Cuba. This was right in America's backyard and no American President would stand for any meddling there.

He had suggested to Nicholas to send his houseboat to be re-fitted at a recommended boatyard and had personally seen to it that some extra gismos be added, at the same time. He thought that this pleasure boat, on the Thames, would be the perfect means of surveillance, right on their doorstep, so to speak.

There was a knock and Carole put her head round the door. "Is that all for this evening Sir Charles? I rather wanted to get off early tonight. I have changed my accommodation temporarily and have to re-organise my new home. My present address has been left, with the downstairs office.

"That's rather sudden, isn't it? Can we be of any assistance to you. I thought you lived on the river."

"Well yes, that was my temporary home, but the boat has had to go for repair work, so I had to rehouse in rather a hurry."

"Oh, well I do hope your new home is satisfactory, as we can sometimes find accommodation at short notice for special employees and I wouldn't want you to feel you had no other choice."

"Thank you, Sir Charles. That is very kind of you. It is good to know."

"When you come in after the weekend I shall have a couple of assignments waiting for you." He said to deflect any conversation about the boat.

"Do you ever see your old lady friend these days?"

"Well yes, occasionally. Of course, when Janice left for Geneva, I gave up my tenancy of the flat-share, but when my neighbour Anna, came home from the hospital, she was very frail and has needed nursing ever since. I do like to check up on her now and then as she had been so kind to me."

"That's splendid, it's good to hear that old friends are valued even if they caused you trouble at the time." Said Sir Charles, with just a touch of irony. "Well off you go now as there will be nothing urgent this evening!"

As she turned to go, Sir Charles was eyeing her speculatively. Yes. Now he had a plan, feeling rather pleased with himself. Yes, he had a plan. He repeated to himself. A very good plan and had the perfect couple to carry it out.

He set his blotter tidily in front of him and put his pens away in the front drawer, and rested his hands on the polished mahogany of the large desk. After a minute's contemplation he stood up, recovered a mackintosh and placed a bowler hat firmly on his head. A smile lingered on his face. Yes, a very satisfactory end to the day.

CHAPTER 6

The Invitation

Two days later, Carole received a formal invitation to be a guest at a Summer Garden Party at Wimple House at Orchard Hill, near Richmond and it bore the crest of the Romanovs. She searched it for clues as to the identity of the sender, but could only surmise that Anna had sent it to her. This was to be held on 14th July and was to be a celebration of Bastille Day. Many of the émigrés had strong French connections and this was their major commemorative event of the French Revolution.

Carole decided to visit her old neighbour Anna, to enquire as to her health and get some information on the event.

Anna had seemed much more fragile since returning from the hospital. Her involvement in passing the Romanov pearls to Nicholas, had been kept secret by Carole and Janice. They had realised that Anna did not want her financial support of the rescue of Stefan Baronski, to be known by the officers at the Russian Embassy. Support for the aspirations of the Chevaliers de Ruissé was regarded as seditious by the present Soviet Regime. For they were supporting the dream of many of the émigrés who fled

Russia during the Revolution.

She waited until the weekend, not wishing to knock on Anna's door in the evening. Entering the downstairs lobby, she was hailed by the caretaker, Mr. Brestov, who smiled at her.

"Hello Carole, nice to see your smiling face again."

"Is Anna in?" She enquired.

"Yes, I think so. She will be glad of a visit because she doesn't get out much now."

It felt strange to be back in the building that had been her home with Janice last year, and the memories of that time came flooding back. This was when she had met Nicholas and the part he had played in taking the pearls gave her pangs of longing for his return Carole skipped up the stairs and knocked on Anna's door.

It was a bright sunny day and she had enjoyed her walk but she was willing to take a turn round the gardens if Anna felt strong enough.

The door was opened by a rather dour, long faced lady who recognised Carole. "Oh, do come in, you will be quite a tonic for Anna today."

"Hello." She said and walking into the large airy room, found Anna sitting upright in a straight-backed chair, holding a silver handled walking stick.

"Hello, my dear, so kind of you to visit such an old lady again." She said in a frail voice.

The silver teapot and milk set, was immediately brought into service and Carole handed over some French tarts she had purchased at the patisserie.

"Now tell me, my dear, what have you been doing? My life here is so uneventful and you are like a breath of fresh air for me." Anna enquired.

"Well, I thought you might like to take a turn in the garden if Gretcha approves?"

"That's fine, Anna is feeling well today and the summer air will do her good." Said her solemn faced nurse.

A new lift had been installed in the six months since Carole had lived in their flat and they used this to take Anna downstairs in a wheelchair, wrapped in a warm coat and scarf. "How the seasons change. Isn't it lovely out here? She exclaimed. Now, tell me all your news I feel so cut off from the world, sitting upstairs all the while."

Carole had received a letter from her flat-mate Janice since her last visit to Anna and she diverted her with news of Geneva, where Janice was working for the embassy. It was a city she knew from her youth and entertained Carole with anecdotes of her time there.

"You must go to see her, you will love Geneva, such a clean city and so cosmopolitan." Anna enthused.

"I must thank you for your invitation to the Summer Garden Party next month. I am sure it will be lovely." Carole remembered to say when there was a pause in Anna's reminiscence.

"Oh, my dear, I haven't sent any invitations. I am rather restricted, as you can see, and I haven't managed to get out to any party, since my accident." She hesitated." Have you seen anything of that lovely young man you went to the Ball with, that you were so excited about?"

Carole looked her straight in the eye and said drily. "No, I haven't, but I rather thought you might have heard or seen him?"

Anna looked back at her, innocent of eye, and said. "Well I haven't, but I did hear that his father had managed to get to England after many trials and tribulations. Did he tell you his family story?" Carole nodded without speaking.

"His father spoke out too bravely about conditions in Russia and paid the price by being sent to the Gulag." Continued Anna. "I understand that he was recently 'released' and has been given asylum in Britain. He's a broken man, of course, and may never fully recover. So sad, I have had my time but he was struck down in his prime. He is still young enough to take up the reins of his former activities, if he is ever fit enough to do so.

He had a very fine brain but whether he will remain a broken man, or have enough fire still, to speak out, we shall see."

Carole was beginning to perceive that there were lots of reasons why Nicholas had not come to her.

She walked Anna back to her flat and was thoughtful after their talk. A lot had been said that was new to her, and she was in a sad mood when she let herself into her temporary home.

Everything here was the height of sophistication and, exploring the bedroom, Carole had discovered the dressing table with all her own things laid out on the surface. In the wardrobe, hung her own clothes, which had all been on the boat, and when turning back the coverlets she found a beautiful silk and lace nightdress and negligee set which was all wrapped up in tissue paper and carried a label from Harrods. Soberly she had wondered about the 'kept woman' appellation but her recent talk with Anna changed her view on this and gave her hope that this was the way Nicholas was wooing her.

She had felt inclined to find some other accommodation but her instinct told her that Nicholas was trying to maintain contact and, if she left, that tie would be broken, for he would have no idea where she was working now.

CHAPTER 7

River Barbecue

On the last week in June Carole had decided to spend a weekend in Worcestershire with her parents and had heard from her friend Peter that he would be down there as well, so she was looking forward to having a carefree moment with some of her childhood chums.

The weather was set fair and she thought it was time that all her personal memories should be left behind, and hoped her visit would ease her parents' sorrow.

The train to Wales had been fast and she felt free of worries as soon as the countryside was slipping past She found herself eager to explore old haunts instead of the dread experienced at the reminders of her dead brother and her parents' grief.

Peter Swayne had said he would meet her train and he was there at Evesham Station to pick her up.

"I've got lots of ideas for the weekend Carole.

Do you have anything special in mind?"

"Not really, Peter." She said.

"I suppose we ought to pop into 'The Angel' to see Margaret and perhaps some of the crowd that may still be around." He said.

"That's perfect Peter."

"And we must get on that river sometime. Perhaps we should make it a pub crawl upriver to Piddleham. There's cider aplenty to sample and maybe your mum has some home brewed damson wine." Peter enthused.

They laughed gaily, each in their own way trying to exorcise the ghost of the past. Carole had decided that ghost or not, she would live her life for her dead brother, and would not bury his memory and grieve for all time. Her parents had done enough of that already and she would not let herself feel guilty for his own misdeeds. He had been driving when he landed in that watery ditch and he alone was responsible for drinking too much.

They parked the car in the Market Square and arm in arm they laughingly entered the lobby of The Angel and went into the public bar. All was as she remembered it and behind the counter, sure enough, was their friend of old, Margaret Merrydown.

"Maggie." Squealed Carole, disturbing the quiet air of the Saturday trade. Both girls embraced and started to chatter.

Peter put his arm around Carole in a proprietorial

manner and dragged Carole away from her friend.

Now girls, let's get things organised. Who of our friends are we likely to find this weekend? We are thinking of doing something on the river and we need to know numbers." They argued agreeably for some time but settled for a trip up river, and a barbecue/swim opposite The Anchor, agreeing to meet after Margaret had finished her duties.

Peter and Carole took their drinks onto the terrace overlooking the river and exclaimed with delight at their treasured view of Bredon Hill.

They did not glance around at any other drinker in the bar but the man sitting with his elderly father heard and saw them come in. He leaned back into the inglenook, keeping the right side of his face deep in shadow, but continued to observe the noisy scene at the bar.

They looked an infectiously cheerful couple and seemed at home here. His heart contracted, seeing how relaxed the young woman and the young man were with each other and his heart turned to stone. How could he compete with such youthful exuberance He felt so old, for his care for his sick father had taken its toll of his spirits and he realised that his moment with Carole might be slipping away.

Carole and Peter finished their drinks and came back

into the bar but did not glance at the 'snuggery'. They walked purposefully to the front door and turned right along the High Street and right again down a small lane to a small village green and knocked on the front door of the house on the left.

"Good morning, Mrs. S. I've brought your lovely daughter safely home." And he planted a kiss on her mother's cheeks.

"Hello Peter, 'long time, no see.' Are you home for good now?"

Carole threw her bag onto the sofa, as though coming in from school, and her mother frowned. "Put your bag upstairs Carole and I will get you both a cup of coffee. Have you eaten yet?"

Carole heard the disapproval in her mother's voice but felt rather rebellious so continued to sit on her chair. At that moment, a large tabby cat walked into the room and jumped onto her lap. She was surprised to find a cat in this house and said, "Mother, where did you get this cat? I didn't think you liked them."

"Well this one likes me. I can't get rid of him. He just walks in, without a 'by your leave,' and jumps onto your bed to sun himself. I don't feed him, but he likes to live here sometimes. He actually belongs to our new neighbours, but I think that our house has more sun, especially as the garden is rather overgrown next door. The old man seems to be a semi-invalid and the son comes and goes. So, they don't seem to spend much time in the garden. I think he feels more at home here."

"Well I like him." Carole said forlornly. "He very much reminds me of a cat I had in London."

After coffee, Peter jumped up and interrupted, "I must go Mrs. S. but I will be back when I have fixed up the use of the boat."

The weekend flew and all the old haunts were visited. There seemed not enough time, to do all that they planned, but she felt refreshed by the easy way they all came together.

All the youthful activity that filled the house was tolerated by her father and mother but it did not seem to give them any pleasure, to see Carole in better health than they had seen her at Christmas. Their own woes seemed to be paramount, all the time.

Carole had woken early, after their evening on the river Avon, and had taken herself down to gaze at this river of her childhood and soak up all the familiar sights and sounds. She had heard the lark rising over the meadows on the opposite bank and its soaring melody lifted her spirits for the day to come. She turned downstream and followed the customary path through her neighbours' garden and on towards The Angel. She heard the weir burbling downstream and saw the Corn Mill to her right.

Her world was changing, she reflected, but here everything was as it had always been. She could not see that even her own small part of England would be changed forever by progress, and the new motorway North to South of the town.

CHAPTER 8

A Sleepless Night

Nicholas had spent the weekend in frustrated anger at his cowardice. He had come to terms with his altered appearance and, indeed, the scar. sustained, when trying to get his father out of Russia, was slowly becoming less vivid. The beard that was growing was gradually covering much of it, but he must be reconciled to the fact that this face would never look the same again.

He reasoned that the needs of his father were paramount. That he would contact Carole as soon as Stefan's immediate wants were attended to, but also knew, deep down, that he feared her pity. Now, the game of hide and seek had lasted too long. That she had understood the messages, he did not doubt, but perhaps she also saw them as a game, and was picking up the life she had before meeting him.

Nicholas acknowledged that he understood these sturdy country boys. After all, weren't their lives similar to his own childhood on the farm of his uncle in Russia. He began to identify with this new land with its fertile soil. His frustration grew as the weekend progressed as the friends of her childhood gathered around her. Many of the young men who had gone away to do their National Service, had returned to the village to become farmers, market gardeners, corn merchants and teachers, and they had found a jewel in their midst with this beautiful blonde sophisticate, who flashed her sparkling eyes at them all and laughingly fended off their amorous advances.

Right in front of his eyes, as the party took to the river, with their boats laden with beer and picnic and thick rugs and paraphernalia to enjoy a summer night, and he longed to join this happy crowd and claim her as his own.

Later, his frustration was at fever pitch. After tossing and turning, Nicholas had heard them returning downstream by the sound of their twin stroke engines.

He had heard their exaggerated shushing as they tried to make their silent, tipsy way, back to Carole's home. The windless night and calm water carried their voices clearly into his bedroom in the pre-dawn air.

There was a clatter of a bucket, and again a shushing and giggles from the girls, Then, a silence so palpable that Nicholas, in his anguish, dared not look out of the window He feared to catch sight of Carole in a long goodbye with that fat faced, frizzy haired fop with two flat feet, who had danced attendance upon her in such a proprietorial way. All weekend!

He finally slept and was surprised to find his father at his bedside with a cup of tea, made the Russian way, with a slice of lemon, and he saw that it was almost midday.

"Come on bone head, you have had all the sleep you need for today."

"Oh, Papa Stefan, I'm sorry. I was woken in the night by the midnight revelers and I have overslept." His father looked at him keenly, as he caught a strange note in his son's voice. Surely, he was over-reacting. Was he jealous? That girl, who had landed with her followers at lunchtime yesterday, had certainly been appreciated by Stefan and he noticed that Nicholas thought so too, but he could not account for such vehemence in his son's voice.

"Come on, up you get, perhaps you could walk me along the riverbank. Perhaps I should think of getting a dog, Nico. A bit of walking will soon restore my feeble muscles."

Nicholas looked at his father doubtfully. Perhaps he was fussing too much.

"Alright, Papa Stefan, but have you eaten any breakfast?" And he hurried to make himself ready.

They walked down the garden and left through their neighbours' garden and upstream through meadows, where cows were feeding and all was tranquil around them. In the distance was a mill and across the meadow the sound of rattling rigging broke the somnolence of the air.

While they were walking, Stefan explained to Nicholas that he had somehow received a call this morning from his dear friend Tasha, whom he knew had taken care and educated his son during his absence. It had lifted his spirits to hear from his friend. He was so indebted to him for his care of the fine young man that Stefan had grown to love once more. Not as the child of his memory but for the brave, kind and handsome man he had become. He did not see the scar that Nicholas had sustained as it was nobly won and no man, was ever prouder, of the deeds that had produced that mark of manhood.

He had begun to suspect, as his strength had returned, that Nicholas was perhaps hiding from the world and that he was too sensitive to his changed appearance. If Nicholas had been able to be objective, he would have seen, that now that the rawness was going from the wound, he was still a very attractive man.

Gone was the softness of youthful promise and sparkle. Here was a man, fully formed with that badge of experience that many a man would envy and many a woman, Stefan now suspected, would find irresistible.

No, thought Stefan, I can't let him hide away here, and Tasha had given him the perfect opportunity to change things.

"Yes, he has invited us to stay with them for a week or so and I feel I am now able to see something more of this lovely country. And perhaps hear more of the horses."

"Oh, I am glad that you are getting stronger and feel

able to see something more of the world. I also have to be in London for a fortnight so that is a splendid suggestion."

They had been walking slowly but had drawn closer to the Mill that had been in the distance and they could see that there was more activity. There were boats of all kinds around the building and it seemed a focus for sailing boats, that were taking to the water, in what appeared the beginnings of a race. Nicholas awoke to the possibility of meeting Carole, and drew his father around to retrace their steps. He had thought that there was less chance of a meeting after last night's revelries but he saw that it was 11.30 a.m. and most people had stirred by now.

The church bells were ringing from over the fields as they turned away and returned to their cottage.

CHAPTER 9

The Pain of Lost Love

Carole returned to the office on Monday morning feeling rested and at peace with the world.

Sir Charles seemed in a very businesslike mood and handed her a portfolio. "This is for you to study and memorise. I know that you are going to the Bastille Day Celebrations at Wimple House on Orchard Hill next month, and it will be very useful to us, for you to observe the people there. I shall expect a full report on personnel on your return."

"In the meantime," Sir Charles said crisply, "I shall appoint Ian Duncan to act as escort. It seems a harmless summer entertainment but the title says it all, 'Bastille Day Celebrations.' Make no mistake, there will likely be many revolutionary undertones with both Communists and Royalists mingling with their French sympathizers and is an ideal venue for intrigues."

"It is a revolutionary cauldron and a watcher's paradise." He added.

She couldn't help but smile and thought of her hours of bird watching and their different characteristics. Not a bad analogy, she thought as she remembered their fights over territory.

It was all very serious in Whitehall and the day flew past.

In her lunchtime, she decided to go into The Tate to see the Picasso exhibition and 'mock up' on her French Impressionists. She loved this building on her doorstep and had often strolled there in her lunchtime, but usually she went to see the 'Turners' and all the boat pictures that she could better understand. She had been instructed in such artists whilst at Birmingham Art School and her mind was receptive to such modern images.

She had had furious debates, in the past, with her father over Picasso and his contemporaries. She had defended the avant-garde view. Now, looking afresh at so many like images, she was not so sure, until she came upon a copy of Guernica and she stood transfixed. What an image of the horrors of war! His genius sprang off the wall and could not be denied. Carole was familiar with Nash and the other war artists at the War Museum, with all their depictions of desolation, but here was war in all its visceral crudity and she could almost smell the blood from the monotoned images that had no hint of colour to aid her senses, except a single flash of red.

With her new-found awareness of foreign politics, Carole felt the reality of war as she had never been able to envisage it before and the discord and threats that the

Nuclear Age had brought were now right at the heart of her existence. She walked slowly and thoughtfully back along the Embankment and settled to her reading.

There was a glittering array of people that she had to memorise, with all their detailed likes and dislikes. There would be several French dignitaries amongst the guests and some were the people she had known from Christmas. She also saw that Sheila Fielding and Barbara Borgen were amongst the lesser names. She sighed and remembered the last time they had met. She hoped that no particulars of her part in the 'pearls affair' had reached their ears and that they offered simple friendship and not some twist in the plot that had been hatched.

It was sufficient to have to interpret Nicholas's messages without being drawn further into their affairs! She thought ruefully.

****

That evening she was invited to supper with Ian who had volunteered to take her to the pictures by way of any awkwardness that might develop between them. So far, Ian had not spoken to Carole but he knew that she had been the flat-mate of Janice, who had helped in the affair of the 'string of pearls,' so he was pleased to be partnered with her on their assignment.

Ian Duncan had been with the Foreign Office for 12 months and was a very conscientious member of the team.

Very bright and very serious, he had been more successful in work than in love and this pairing frightened him to death. His dates so far, were with work colleagues, but they had been strictly in the 'line of duty.'

Ian had secretly rather liked the look of Janice, and she had been a perfect partner for him at the 'Ministerial Dinner' they had attended. He had just been plucking up his courage to ask her out properly, when she had been posted to Geneva and his chance had disappeared.

He was a gawkish young man and was at his best in a smart suit, but his assured manner, when carrying out his duties, stopped short with the girls. His reticence there, meant that he never showed his feelings enough to encourage them. Put him in a pair of beach shorts and his hollow chest and apparent lack of sporting prowess was fully exposed. His only experience of girls had been strictly the pecuniary variety which had satisfied his needs but had left him with very little rapport to call upon.

Tonight, he was to have the hottest date in the office and couldn't believe his luck. He had suggested that they found somewhere to eat on the Kings Road, as he had heard that it was lively there, but she had vetoed that and suggested somewhere in Leicester Square where the film version of 'West Side Story' was having rave reviews. and Ian hoped that a film afterwards would be to her liking.

They found a small Italian place in Greek Street and the friendliness of the staff made up for his embarrassing pauses in the conversation. "Where do you come from Ian, I don't detect any trace of an accent?"

He bristled as, of course, he had an accent, the correct one that everybody should aspire to. The Queen's English. He thought rather pompously. "I come from Sussex but my schooling was in Sherborne, Dorset, and my family come from Scotland. So, if anything, I suppose I might have picked up a bit of a southern drawl but I hope that is not detectable here in London." And he frowned thinking of such a horror.

The silence lengthened as Carole thought desperately of another opening gambit. "My home is in Worcestershire."

"Oh, where the apples and pears, plums and cherries come from." He said, thinking to make a joke, but Carole answered robustly. "It's not just market garden country. We boast two spa towns and the River Avon puts us at the heart of Shakespeare Country, even though Stratford is actually just over the county border."

She said proudly as an afterthought. No one was going to disparage her Midland roots.

"Yes, and I suppose that makes you a Brummie." He said in mock accent.

'How dare he!" She thought hotly, as the evening went from bad to worse.

By the time they had finished the meal she was ready to go home but knew that this was really a business evening and, as such, must be polite. Carole was at every turn, comparing him to Nicholas. Her irritation was not Ian's fault but because of her own heartache.

They just scraped into the final showing of the film, which was a bit mushy, he thought, but everyone seemed to be absorbed so he glanced at Carole.

To his acute discomfort, Ian could see that she was crying and was deeply affected by the story. When the lights came up he saw that she was sobbing quietly in her seat. Quickly he shielded her from onlookers and said, "Don't get upset by a silly movie. It's only a story, it isn't real." He expostulated, and Carole's sobs became louder.

"Look." He said, as his discomfort grew, "Let's go and have a coffee before we go back to your place. I'm sure that will make you feel better." And at every suggestion the sobs grew louder.

What was the matter with the girl? These women were a complete mystery to him with their exaggerated sentiment.

By now he was in an acute state of embarrassment and he couldn't wait to see her home. "Please, Ian, can we skip the coffee, I really don't feel very well and would rather just go home."

"That's fine." He agreed immediately and they rushed

for the night bus back to Victoria. Poor Ian, he really didn't know anything. An opportunist, would have exploited her heightened emotional state, to give her 'special comfort' and, who knows where that would have ended.

Poor Ian indeed, the young Lothario went home completely relieved to have discharged his duties to her and walked quickly back to his flat.

CHAPTER 10

Romantic Plans

Nicholas had left his father with his dear guardian in Hampshire and had gone straight to London. He had to see to the boat, and return it to Chelsea, and check in to see Sir Charles. So, the decision his father had taken was useful, without having to lie to him in any way. His father had also been persuaded to come to the Bastille Day Celebrations, which had been a more difficult puzzle for him to explain.

He was to be on official duty at this event but must equally concern himself with his father's welfare. There was the added problem of facing people who had known him during the Christmas Soirée and some of them had scores to settle.

He was pleased to see that the boat was almost ready. Its past life was erased and a newer and faster boat had emerged from the re-fit. The electronics on board were as up to date as a Formula One car and a little touch of comfort had been added to the cabin. He remembered his nights of passion with Carole and was determined that no cleats or shackles impeded their nocturnal comfort! He sighed at the thought and quickly finished the business with the boat builder.

They soon launched the boat from the gantry and he tested the engines. The sound of them was almost non-existent even though there was increased horsepower in the engine specification. The engine purred round the little boatyard inlet while he tested its new maneuverability and was pleased with her handling.

He opened the throttle to test its speed whilst watching for any police launch. It certainly handled well and Nicholas felt confident at out-running most of the craft on this part of the river. It had yet to be tested in the rougher waters of the North Sea!

He turned the craft downstream and, against the flow of the tide, made his way towards Parliament. He had hoped to finish his business with Sir Charles before the office workers left, so that he could secure his berth at Chelsea Harbour before Carole returned. He cursed under his breath seeing that the upstream flow of the river was more difficult to negotiate, as he had still to master the handling of his re-fitted craft. He chided himself at his impatience. There was no need to hurry.

Still his agitation rose at the thought of his delays and procrastination. His responsibility to his father was rapidly diminishing, as Stefan had been keen to take his place in the world again. He must not delay a meeting with Carole any longer. Having made his decision, he was eager to renew their friendship.

He maneuvered his craft to the steps by Westminster

Bridge, and secured it firmly to the iron rings in the wall, next to the pleasure boat jetty and jumped up the steps, two at a time, onto the Embankment.

He was let into the Government building as before and was soon in Sir Charles's office.

"Ah, good evening Mr. Baron, I was expecting you earlier so that I could introduce you to your partner. We have a new operative who has been well trained and you may have full confidence in their ability to handle most craft. However other duties call and I will not be able to introduce you until tomorrow."

Nicholas left with relief, hoping to make up lost time, so it was getting on for 7.00 p.m. when he finally docked below Chelsea Harbour and secured the painter to the rings. He also padlocked chains to underneath the jetty. He didn't want to lose his new beauty to a seafaring thief!

He went down the hatchway and surveyed the new re-fit. No stove was there to warm the cabin. Instead, all the heating came from an oil-fired boiler, and long tubes situated behind the seating gave off thermostatically controlled warmth.

No longer was the kettle, with its cheerful whistle, heated by the stove, but was connected to a new electrical generator.

All trace of his messenger system was gone and he

smiled as a new chapter was about to begin.

He had left Carole safe and comfortable in Tasha's flat, hadn't he? Now he was ready to face her, and was full of confidence that he would win her back.

The hours ticked past as he waited for her return, fretting that something had befallen her. He didn't see the boats still chugging their way up river. He didn't notice the lights of late evening begin to light up the Embankment. He didn't feel the cold breeze flattening the waves on the river as it rushed back to sea. Ducks flew overhead upstream to summer roosts but he took no notice of their honking flight.

The only things of interest were the unlit 4th floor window which overlooked the street, and the route from the City.

Many commuters hurried on their way along the Embankment, some glancing at the man standing there, now with his storm jacket buttoned against the buffeting wind. Most, just hurried by, and still no sight of Carole. He was not conscious of hunger, even though it was many hours since he had eaten.

All his well-laid plans were in vain. Nicholas despaired that she had gone away, but where? What a fool he had been, what selfish arrogance, to think that he could just come back into her life at his choosing.

He had good reasons, it was true. But also, knew that

it was vanity that had made him hesitate about her reception of his altered appearance.

Now he cursed himself for thinking that she would wait forever. Nicholas knew only too well the heights her passion could reach, and here he was, leaving her alone to find consolation or, and here he paused and accepted the possibility, even another love, who would cherish her forever.

He heard Big Ben in the distance chime the midnight hour and decided that she would not come. He glanced once more towards Westminster and saw two figures hurrying along the pavement, and by the light of the street lamp, saw Carole's long blonde hair.

He turned to face the river as his heart flared with jealousy seeing that she was with an escort. What was he doing, standing there like some prowler in the night, and knew that this approach had been crass and demented. He could not meet her in this way.

Whilst standing there by the statue of the Dolphin, he saw that the escort had given Carole a most cursory goodbye. Had he misinterpreted her evening out? It certainly didn't show any sign of romance to it, and hope returned.

But still Nicholas hesitated, as he realised how frightening his appearance, on her doorstep, would be at this time of night.

He revised the course of action and decided to send a bouquet of flowers to her flat so that she should be prepared for a visit. He arose with the dawn but had no eyes for its beauty as he hurried to the early flower sellers stall. He pinned a short note to the wrapping and took them to the lobby of Dolphin Square for early delivery and went off to find a locals' café, with renewed hope, suddenly feeling ravenously hungry.

CHAPTER 11

Partnership

Carole took the lift to her flat after the evening out with Ian. Well, what an evening! She thought. How did I manage to endure it? Her opinion of men took a complete dive, when she thought of his crass behavior and unsympathetic reaction to her distress. When she had time to think, she wondered whether the reaction to the film. had been rather excessive? The tragic end for the star-crossed lovers brought home the hopelessness of her dreams. She must put them aside and get on with her life.

She was soon to be tested in her first real assignment, so she had better toughen up. She awoke early with a splitting headache and swollen eyes and her beauty of yesterday was hard to see. She splashed cold water over her eyelids and hoped that her appearance improved. Drat it! I have to meet my new partner today Let's hope it is not going to be Ian. Oh no, not that oaf, she thought. I shall have to put up with him at Bastille Day. That will be enough!

She decided that a brisk walk was called for and left the flat 15 minutes early to allow her to walk to work. She had just stepped into the lift, when the caretaker came through the door with a large bouquet of flowers. As he opened the doors to the second lift, the note attached was dislodged and slipped between the lift and the landing, disappearing down the slit He placed the flowers on the doorstep of her flat and went downstairs again, just as Carole disappeared out of the building.

The fresh breeze and bright sunlight of the July day, brought Carole to a better state of mind and she set off to meet her new partner and assignment. She knew already, that some of the characters in her dossier would be at the Garden Party, but could not imagine what her surveillance might entail.

The night had brought rain to the city, which had left the air heavy with perfume. All the pavements were fresh and new, for just a few hours at least, before the detritus of footfall covered them again.

She entered the office building at the Foreign Office and went up the stairs to Sir Charles's room. She missed the cheerful greeting of her former concierge, Joe Southgate, at Messrs. Bailey, Bailey, & Wagstaff, and wondered whether his family were well. They had been very caring people when she needed a friend and she did not intend to forget them. Perhaps when this assignment was over she would pay them a visit. Good friends were rare and she did not intend to lose sight of such a lovely family.

As she entered his office, Sir Charles already had a visitor sitting with his back to her.

"Ah, Carole, I think you already know your new partner, so I need hardly introduce you, except to give Nicholas your new name. Allow me to introduce Miss Carole Penny. Carole, you already know Nicholas as Mr. Baron but for this assignment, he will be Mr. Barr, Mr. Nicholas Barr."

They stared at each other in astonishment and Sir Charles laughed at his little joke, realising that he had dumbfounded them both. "Perhaps you will take Nicholas to your office and give him an idea where we have reached in our investigation and he can take you to the Embankment to show you the mechanics of his new boat.

As she left his office, Carole found that her knees were shaking and it took all her willpower to cross the carpeted floor into her office. She felt Nicholas put his hand under her arm and steer her through the door, shutting it firmly behind him. He put his arms around her and drew her to his chest in a loving embrace as if he would never let her go. Her pliant figure was half fainting until she mustered her anger sufficiently to fight him. She pounded his chest with her fists. "How dare you, how dare you. Why have you come back into my life but not come to me of your own free will?"

"You didn't know it would be me that you are to work with and I did not know it was you. But this meeting is long overdue and I don't understand why you have left me hoping you would return but still stayed away, watching me!"

He backed away in astonishment at her raw, angry

protest, and he put his hands on her shoulders and shook her slightly. "Carole, Carole, look at me, look at me." As he stilled her tirade. They looked at each other eye to eye and he felt the anger drain away from her. He was surprised to see no echoing surprise in her eyes and certainly no revulsion.

"Do you think that I wanted to stay away from you, do you think I haven't longed to hold you in my arms like I have just done. Good God Carole, just look at me please. What have I to offer now, to a lovely, vital, young woman? I have come back to England, a husk of the person I was, and I thought that I should leave you to lead your life without me, but I found that I couldn't do it."

"That is why I watched at your doorstep last night, awaiting your return. To tell you I love you, I love you, but can you still love me, this ugly, battered wreck of a man who feared to put you to that test." He bowed his head in abject despair and the silence lengthened.

Carole had held her breath while he had given his impassioned reasoning. Now she took a long intake of air, to steady herself to answer. She knew that all these things that he had told her, rang true. She must choose her words carefully, if they were to have any future together.

"Nicholas, look at me. You asked me to look at you, well, now look at me." She paused. "Do you think I love you for what you look like? Yes of course, I would be a fool to say anything else. But the marks of a life doing honourable things will always change a person's looks. Evil is always uglier than ugliness in pursuit of good, for that is a mark of honour."

"I have heard something of your sacrifices in bringing your father to England. I will always love you for that."

She repeated. "Nicholas, oh Nicholas, I love you and what you are and how you look will not alter that so no more drama over it. She said crisply. We have a job to do together, I believe." She landed a kiss lightly onto his scar and surrendered to his embrace.

Sir Charles sat drinking his tea. He had suggested to the tea lady that Carole was too busily engaged for tea, to prevent her chatty entry upon, what he surmised was, a rather fiery debate going on. He hoped that this partnership might prove to be very successful.

In his world of marionettes, he had tied his threads, attached to these two, young people, and would watch how they would dance.

As the master puppeteer, he had nurtured their talents and tested their loyalties in the months since their parting. Now he was ready to set the dancers in motion to mesmerize the crowds and draw their secrets from them.

Yes, he was pleased, very pleased, he thought, as he sensed their attachment to each other. Yes, he thought, that loyal soldier had been through a life-changing reality in the past months but now he was entitled to a little bit of heaven. He paused, and thought wryly of their task. All in the line of duty, of course!

CHAPTER 12

Cutty Sark

Carole and Nicholas walked out of the building and towards the wharf.

They walked side by side down the alley to the river, not touching, but an invisible thread still bound them.

As they came out onto the Embankment, Nicholas turned and grabbed her hand, steering them precariously across the road.

"There you are!" He said proudly. "Our new home. Isn't she a beauty with her new coat of paint? Wait till you see her inside!"

She smiled blissfully at him and thought how much younger he sounded already in his eagerness to show off the boat. The break in tension too, had allowed them to put their own lives on hold, and returned them to their task at hand.

He clambered down the footfalls to the river and jumped the last yard into the boat and turned to help Carole down. She was already nearly there but she allowed herself to jump down into his waiting arms. There was a pause as he felt the warmth of her and landed a light kiss on her cheek before saying briskly. "We have a lot to do today, so we had better make haste. You'll find everything you need for a sea trip in the cabin, so let's get started."

He busied himself casting off, and she retrieved the fenders, stowing them neatly in the bows, then entered the cabin and threw her handbag onto one of the swabs. She laughed in delight at the change that had been wrought and the luxury she saw, made her shake her head in disbelief.

She picked up the black stretch trousers and top and pulled them on and reached for the all-weather jacket, spilling some of the contents of the dossier with her name on it, laid on the bunk. She bent to retrieve the contents and picked up a thin strip of packaged pills and looked hard at them. Well, this was something she should definitely use after her recklessness at Christmas.

In the six months of her training she had become a more worldly-wise young woman. The training had been thorough, especially as she was well aware of her role as the honeypot, in this enterprise.

By the time she had changed into the suitable clothes, they were well on their way down river. She was just in time to see her old office, behind the Customs House, before they passed under Tower Bridge and beyond. The river was alive with all the Lighters passing up and down the river, with their cargoes of goods from the four corners of the earth.

It was wonderful to be out on the stream, to watch the docks slide by. Although having been to Greenwich before, she had not been on the river during a working week. She was conscious of how skillfully Nicholas needed to steer their craft, with such a lot of activity around them. She came up onto the deck and joined him at his side quietly, not touching. She could see that he needed to concentrate to avoid all the traffic plying its way up and down and cross-crossing from shore to shore.

Sometime later she could see Greenwich coming up on their starboard bow and she admired the grand Georgian buildings of the Admiralty and the tall masts of the 'Cutty Sark'. How proud she stood in her fastness. How thrilling it must have been to sail before her mast in those great races, to bring back her cargo of tea. To think that such grace and power was so short-lived, as this graceful sailing ship was superseded by the iron clad monsters that followed her. Thus, bringing more certainty, to the timing of the new tea crop arriving in England.

What a sight she must have been with all her canvasses at full stretch. They looked at each other as they left the 'Cutty Sark' behind them and grinned in perfect understanding. He could see that their knowledge and love of the sea was in perfect accord and he knew that she was thinking the same thoughts as hundreds of others at the sight of that maritime majesty.

Before long they had left the docks behind on the port

bow and Nicholas at last gave her some real attention. "Here, do you want a turn of the wheel? Throttle her gently but otherwise, steady as you go." She nodded and he relinquished the wheel to her, whilst he went below to make some lunch and put on the newfangled kettle. He had been dubious about this, as he missed the company of the old one, with its cheerful whistle, but he had to admit that it did the job so much quicker.

The river had widened considerably by the time his big cheese sandwiches were ready and the tea made, and he stepped into the cockpit just as they were passing flat marshes on either side. "There's a small jetty ahead to starboard. Steer her in and we'll anchor up for lunch, before we open her up, out to sea."

She was thrilled to hear the confidence in his voice, as to her competence, and she throttled down enough to maintain steerage in the stream, whilst she maneuvered the boat into the shallows, killing speed and reversing to bring her to rest, whilst Nicholas had put all port fenders out and had jumped to secure the boat, making absolutely sure that none of its precious new paint was scratched.

"Whoo, whoo." She could not help shouting in triumph. How's that for a clean landing?"

He smiled back at her with a knowing look. He thought sheepishly that, he must avoid any more personal discussion. He was not about to admit to his knowledge of her abilities and his, nocturnal sleeplessness (in Avonbridge), so replied. "Well your dossier confirms your credentials Ma'am, so I must be able to trust my crew. He said more formally than he wanted to be. What do you think of her? She handles well don't you think?" He said slightly flustered and he continued to ply her with such questions between bites of his cheese sandwiches and gulps of tea.

"Look, the tide is falling fast. She said. If you want to show me her paces we shall have to get off this sandbar quickly." He jumped up, planting a meaningful kiss on her lips, as Carole prepared to caste off.

He started up the engine slowly, just enough to avoid swirling mud in the water, and reversed, trusting to Carole's instincts to jump aboard at the right moment. As she jumped down into the cockpit, with all fenders stowed, he maneuvered the boat out into the stream. That done, he grabbed for Carole and bringing her to his side, gave her a great hug.

"You'll do! We make a fine crew, don't we?" As they both thought of the synchronicity they had displayed there!

Two hours later they had had serious fun while testing the power and steering of their new engines, and were satisfied that they could handle the craft with some accuracy. As the tide began to surge inland they headed back upstream. Letting the tide sweep them up river, they were in no hurry to reach their destination.

It was as if the whole trip had washed away, out to sea, all of their grief, leaving only harmony, and a deep hunger in them. They had little need to satisfy this, watching the passing kaleidoscope of the London skyline around them and savouring the setting sun ahead of their destination. This time Nicholas did see the skeins of ducks, flying inland again, and did hear their needy honking cry. Amen to that. Aroused by his thoughts.

****

They arrived at Westminster Bridge, then Vauxhall and Chelsea as twilight gathered, and Nicholas steered the boat gently into a different berth in the harbour. There were many little tasks to be done, to make them secure, and instinctively they carried out these tasks without need for instructions, until everything was finished. Their meticulously executed tasks hid their sudden shyness, but both knew that this was the moment they had been waiting for since early morning.

Carole went to stow the last fender and was stopped by Nicholas, who drew her up from her task and led her through the galley. They had not put on the kettle. They had not suggested food. All that could wait. Now was the moment to renew their love for one another and it could not be denied.

This, she thought instinctively, is my moment to restore this loving man to himself. She touched his face, running her finger near his scar. He did not need to fear her rejection as she realised, with heightening awareness, that it had a powerful attraction for her. In his ugliness, he was more a man than he had ever been.

****

They lay there naked now, touching and tasting, and her nipples were hard under his hands. Yet still he waited, leading her onto greater arousal, until she rolled over onto him and willed him to taste her breasts as she slowly eased down onto his erect member and heard herself cry out with joy. She swayed backwards and forwards and side to side pressing deeper while he held her buttocks until, with a cry, he held her to him and rolled over to claim her, all passion spent.

The sun was rising over the river again. It was near low water mark by the state of the banks and the flocks of sea birds feeding on the worms but he had no interest in such things. He lay perfectly at peace in a delicious state of torpor. The woman beside him lay with her golden hair across her face breathing softly, her body pale perfection.

He knew that later they had many miles to go upstream but the river's race to the sea had not slackened and there was time to spare before then. His thoughts were of the day ahead, but the change in his life kept creeping into his thoughts and he knew that his body craved with hunger once more.

He knelt at her feet and kissed each toe in turn. His hand traced the line of her foot bones and he kissed the arch of each foot. He began to see her toes curl and proceeded to her ankles and felt her thighs open as he kissed the inside of her knees and continued upwards. He tasted her sweet saltiness and heard her moan softly.

She stretched her arms above her head and wriggled her hips lasciviously, unselfconsciously responding to the tantalizing stimuli. She was fully awake now, and arched her back, thrusting her pelvis upwards. Again, he held back his desire until she had fully awakened and she said in a whisper. "Take me, show how much you need me, show how much you want me, show how much you love me." and his passion held no more restraint. He mounted her urgently and she responded to every thrust with urgent longing of her own, wave upon wave held them in their love rolls to the beach.

The tapping of a seagull on the roof awakened them both to the late hour and they felt the position of the boat had changed with the returning tide.

CHAPTER 13

First Proof of Culpability

Nicholas scurried down the bunk and bit her buttocks lovingly on the way over as he retrieved his clothes. He scrambled to the heads and used the small showerhead that had recently been fitted alongside the toilet, both of which were fed by an overhead closet.

"Heads available." He shouted to Carole, who was beginning to stretch beguilingly but Nicholas had other things on his mind as he prepared to cast off.

****

They reached Richmond in time for breakfast. Carole finished the bread from yesterday with bacon and eggs and beans and sausages with the bread fried in the pan with lashings of brown sauce. They sat outside in the sunshine and ate in silence. Nicholas was tucking into his breakfast with great gusto. He smiled at her with satisfaction. "You know, if I had to choose a country by the breakfast it produced, I would have to choose Britain."

"And what about their women?" She asked archly.

"Oh well, let me see." He paused as though it was difficult to choose. "Em, let me see. Russian women are mostly full bosomed and well rounded, like plums, and full of juice." and he rolled his eyes in mock ecstasy.

She pouted her lips and said nothing but looked mutinously at him.

"And English women? He stopped to consider this, drawing out his answer. "Well I haven't much experience there. Mostly they are tight-arsed and skinny but," And here he paused dramatically, "there is one golden honey blonde with eyes like emeralds and limbs as lithe and… and 'active' as a Caucasian mare!" He finished and laughed as she jumped up and pummeled him with mock angry fists. "Mercy, mercy." He cried as he tried to fend off the blows.

They soon tired of their mock battle and the need for pushing upstream became their priority but there was enough static in the air between them to last until the time was ripe.

They continued upstream to Kingston and negotiated the first lock, waiting their turn, as there was a lot of traffic moving up and down the upper and lower reaches of the Thames. Many of the locks were in a bad state of repair but there seemed many enthusiastic boaters from canoes to motor sail and one or two swanky speedboats around the river island homes.

By 6 o'clock, they had nearly reached their destination above Maidenhead, and they moored up at a coaching inn, with lawns down to the river. Tables and chairs were available for patrons who wished to enjoy the late evening air. The cares of London could be shed as patrons soaked up the sunshine. The sun would be with them for three hours or more, so they had plenty of time to go into the inn and see what they had to offer.

It was a large timbered building, which had little to recommend it from the street, but for those who knew of it, the good food and lovely garden ensured plenty of custom at this time of the year. It provided a discreet meeting place inside, as most of the tables were placed in between high-backed Jacobean styled booths.

There was also a well-stocked Bar and a lovely ingle-nook fireplace, which displayed a huge vase of English roses and lilies, interspersed with gypsophila in the now, empty grate.

They ordered steak and chips and settled back into their own world. She encouraged him to talk about his father and he told her something of his father's condition when he had found him. He was reluctant to tell her about how he had received his wound.

"Let's just say, that certain people didn't want me to leave." He said laconically.

"And how did you get to England?" She asked.

"Oh, I had friends who arranged my passage and we managed to keep our rendezvous with the merchant ship.

"And when did you arrive back in England?" She prompted him.

He hung his head and was silent. He continued. "For many weeks, I needed to help my father regain some of his strength. Also, I was not myself. I had lost a lot of blood and I was in despair about the state of my injury." He faltered and was silent.

He was not now going to work on her sympathy. There was so much to tell her, but not now. There was a lot to be done in the next few days that required concentration and perception, so he needed to put his personal life on hold.

He changed the subject. "How did you come to be working with Sir Charles? Had you been introduced by Janice?"

She paused. Had she been introduced by Janice?' Ah there was a tricky question. She had certainly been brought to his attention by Janice but her involvement in Nicholas' flight, had never been spoken of, and Carole wondered how much he guessed, of her manipulation of his flight.

At last she managed. "He seemed to see some potential and asked me to come and see him after Christmas, which was when Janice was seconded to Geneva. I have been undergoing special training ever since and this is my, first assignment. It seems to be more of an observation exercise than anything. Sir Charles seems to be agitated about something; a leak of vital information very high up in Government"

She stopped and asked. "Do you know anything more about his machinations?"

"Well yes, I think I do, but for the time being, you are better off not knowing. It will cloud your judgment."

They sat back well satisfied with their hearty meal and became aware of their fellow diners. Many were couples like themselves but there was a crowd of men at the bar, talking in louder voices, and the laughter got more raucous, more masculine in its character, until someone said loudly.

"Wow, you should have seen her, she was one sexy bird, not exactly beautiful, but her look, hey it was very much a 'come on', and the way she walked. It had all the chaps eyeing that walk."

"Well he certainly seems to know how to pick them. Isn't he a doctor or something?" Someone interrupted.

"He sure does and he seems to have lots of them in tow, and yes, he is. But I don't know what kind. Some sort of 'shrink' most likely. They are always having these parties up there. Pretty wild I hear."

"Lucky for some." Said another, sharp suited but crumple faced man, of about 55. "Do you think they would notice if we gate-crashed one of their shindigs?"

"Oh, you'll be lucky." Said another. "I think they must be some 'VIP Do's' as I have seen what look like bodyguards up there. They have this wonderful boathouse and they seem to be cavorting in there in the nude. Hey, around a pool."

Someone called for another round of drinks but they had all lapsed in thoughts of their own that the talk had invoked, as these middle-aged men all seemed caught up in the vision of forbidden fruit.

Nicholas suggested to Carole that she use the 'Ladies' and walk provocatively past the group of men appearing to show interest in them, as she went.

He then went up to the bar and ordered another two drinks. "Two brandies please."

One of the fellows at the bar said, as he heard the order. "That's some lovely young woman you are with. Are you on your way to the party up at Basildon? You've certainly picked the jackpot there 'old man'."

Nicholas looked him straight in his bleary eyes and said. "I'm sorry, I don't know what you are insinuating. That LADY is my wife."

The man backed off drunkenly. "I'm sorry, I guess I

thought …" his voice trailed off.

"You guessed what?" Nicholas said in a voice of ice!

"I guess we don't often get ladies as lovely as …your wife." He leered. "Except if they are going to one of the parties up at Basildon. "They have them up there all the time, and there are always lots of lovely young LADIES." He sneered. "No offence meant."

It was obvious that the drunken man did not believe him but had told Nicholas what he wanted to know.

Carole returned to the bar and he turned to her with exaggerated solicitude.

"Oh, there you are darling, shall we have our nightcap." And he steered her to the corner seat.

They were now being watched by all the group at the bar and someone said crudely, "wife, my arse!" and the others laughed knowingly.

Nicholas spoke softly. "Don't react to what they are saying at the bar and smile provocatively at me!"

She did as he said and heard the coarse remarks being exchanged about them. Carole held her smile in place but held tightly to his hand under the table.

Soon he suggested it was time to go and she again looked into his eyes. This time there was a real challenge in her comment. "Anything you want Mr. Barr?" And cast her eyes down demurely.

They walked slowly down the garden towards the riverbank as night descended and they stopped to kiss in the moonlight. The sounds of the night were clear from across the water and bats flew low over its surface. Then, linking hands, they moved towards the river, but were surrounded by mosquitoes, which managed to sting both of them. They ran for cover, laughing, as they made it to the deck and to the shelter of the galley. The spell of the moonlight was shattered as they shook themselves free of the hordes of insects that had followed them.

They sank onto the bunks but Nicholas protested that it had quite undone his manhood. He sat there with arms around his 'wife' and thought 'if only' while he hugged her to him. Just then, the only thing in the world that he needed, was right here, with his arms safely around her.

They lay motionless, breathing in each other's breaths, until they fell asleep to the lapping of the water and the cry of the coot.

CHAPTER 14

Evidence

When the moon had dipped in the sky and the night was at its darkest, Nicholas had disentangled the sleeping woman from his embrace. He began to dress in black jersey and slipped out into the night, belaying the painter and fending off from their mooring, turning upriver at minimum speed. With luck, they would reach their destination in about half an hour, but he was content to let Carole sleep a little while longer.

Soon the high banks were in view and the house they sought stood pale, darkling high above the river.

He turned cautiously downstream, just upstream of the house, and cut the engines to glide silently into the bank. From here he could observe the cottage at the other side of the mooring. They had anchored about 300 yards from a boathouse where sounds of laughter could be heard. He waited several minutes to watch for guards, then shook Carole awake.

"We're here." He said. "But be ready to slip moorings if anything kicks off. If I have any luck, I will be gone about half an hour. Any trouble and I will lay a diversionary trail and meet you down at the Coach and Horses." He looked at her sternly. "You have your gun?" She nodded.

"Don't wait for me if things get sticky, but if you have to, use it. Don't hesitate as some of these folks won't take kindly to exposure."

He disappeared from the hatchway and was gone before she had dressed. She was soon in the jersey and stretch trousers and waiting alert in the protection of the willows higher on the bank. They gave almost complete cover from anyone above looking down on the river, and the re-paint of the hull, to a dark blue, gave no reflection from the boat. Perfect silence was necessary on such a still night.

Twenty minutes passed as she watched the dial on the dashboard. A faint swishing of wet grass was heard and Nicholas was coming back fast towards the boat. She stood ready at the wheel. There was a shout from further away on the terrace, and a dog growled nearer at hand. There was a scuffle near to the bank, another snarl from nearby, then a grunt, and seconds later Nicholas slid down the bank. Carole pressed the engine into life, as he jumped the last yard off the jetty. They were away with a swoosh, with the engine purring like a kitten.

She glanced quickly back at him and saw that he had landed safely, but was in some pain.

"Are you OK?" She asked, alarmed.

He grunted. "I'll be alright, but that Alsatian was a nasty brute and chewed up my arm a bit." He added faintly. "He won't be doing that again."

They docked very quietly, just as dawn was breaking at Windsor, and the majestic battlements of the castle were outlined by the breaking dawn. The swans were unfurling their long necks and shaking out their wings to the approaching sun. In the reeds, the warblers were adding their notes to the dawn chorus of blackbirds, buntings and thrushes, goldfinches and whitethroats, as they filled the air with their magical melody.

Along the river the coots and little grebe were busying themselves in and out of the reed beds with their broods of chicks squawking behind. But all this noise and activity was lost on them as night turned to day for the nocturnal prowlers anchored there.

All along the river the mist was rising, dispelled as the summer sun burnt off all trace of moisture from the ground.

Carole jumped up onto the pontoon and secured the painter whilst Nicholas held the boat steady. He seemed to be having difficulty with his left arm and his voice sounded faint even though she knew their voices were soft anyway. She jumped back down and said crisply.

"Go down into the cabin and I will come and look at

that arm. You should have done this sooner as I can see you are in pain."

"Off now." She urged. "Don't delay. There is nothing left to do here and you need to get out of those clothes into more casual ones. We are fairly exposed in this mooring and, at the moment, we don't want to draw attention to ourselves." And she gently pushed him into the hatchway.

There was a worried frown on her face as she followed him into the cabin and helped him disrobe and she drew a deep intake of breath as the jagged wound on his upper arm was exposed.

She fetched water and the First Aid Kit and saw that he had fallen fast asleep whilst she had been gathering up these necessities.

She worked at cleaning the surface of the wound but saw that the fangs had bitten deep and she was at a loss to know how to clean it properly. She searched for a more drastic solution and bent to the sleeping man.

"I'm sorry but this is going to hurt." She said as she poured a solution of hydrochloric acid and water into the middle of the cut, hoping it would penetrate far enough into the wound. He groaned loudly but did not wake and she gently pushed him down onto the bunk and covered him with a blanket.

She did not bandage the wound, time enough for that,

but lay a gauze underneath his arm to catch any blood seepage and laid another lightly on the surface hoping that his sleep would be deep enough to prevent him turning onto the wound.

Finally, Carole undressed and fell onto the other bunk. Holding his hand, she hoped to be alerted to any movement he might make, and tried to sleep. All her senses were alert now and it was not until the hub-bub of awakening London was fully aroused, that she finally slept.

CHAPTER 15

Adjustments

In Hampshire, Stefan was enjoying the reunion with his dear friends, Tasha and Minka Counter. He was so thankful for all they had done for his son, that it was hard to express.

Several times he had tried to put this into words but would break down in helpless tears halfway through his thanks.

Minka fussed over him with abundant nourishing food, but his fragile state was still unable to cope with anything fancy. It was enough that these friends of his manhood wanted to help.

He was also buoyed up by being able to speak in his mother tongue and this put less strain on his powers of concentration, and progress was accomplished by being bathed in their kindness.

This morning, bright and windless as any July had to offer, he sat with his friends overlooking the downs.

"Well my good friends I hope I can beg another small favour of you.

Tasha brushed away his plea. "Do you need to ask, we are proud to be called a friend. You have sacrificed so much for championing our countrymen. Please how can we help?"

"Well I think it is time I became visible. I have started to write again and I would love to mingle with my countrymen. Will you take me to the Bastille Day Celebrations next weekend? I know that Nicholas has to be there for business purposes, and I do not want to be an encumbrance to him on such an occasion. He should be joining in with the celebrations with his own contemporaries."

"I fear," he continued, "that his changed visage has made him too reclusive. It is not good for him. He must find himself a good woman and give me many grand-children."

"That's just what I say." Exclaimed Minka, bustling around him in motherly fashion. "I have been looking around for both Nicholas and Alex, although they will make their own choice, but we can introduce them to some good Russian stock!" She said stoutly.

The friends continued to make their plans happily in the sunshine.

****

Georgiou Kadinsky was, as usual, strapped for cash. When he was arrested by the River Police, after his attempt to take the pearls from Nicholas, last Christmas, it had done him a good turn. His most pressing creditor had been thwarted by his incarceration. The Police had taken him into custody on suspicion of drug smuggling. It was their opinion that, anyone on the river in the middle of the night, was up to no good, and they were going to investigate his appearance there. His partner in the boat had 'form' and the fact that the driver of the other boat, Nicholas, had got away, probably drowned, might mean that no evidence would be found.

So, at 'Her Majesty's Pleasure,' he had languished in the police cell until news had finally got through to his father. He had delayed the eventuality of a call to his father, as he had thought it useful to lie low. When all the forces of diplomatic immunity were exerted, and he had told his father of his debts, (although not his actual reason for being on the river in the first place), he was left debt free by his father's intervention, but none the wiser for the lesson.

He thought about the pearls that had been lost and blamed Nicholas for taking too long with the hand-over. The fact that faster boats had overhauled them, didn't come into his thinking. Georgiou thought that Nicholas had taken more time over the handover than was necessary, and raged at him, for being the cause of his capture. He had been heavily in debt and his hope of making some cash for the pearls, was now a failure.

Georgiou brooded on his resentment and did not stop to think of his own faults in this matter. His father saw that Georgiou was becoming more resentful and disaffected with England, the country of his adoption, and thought he would make perfect spy material. His father fed his son's resentment deliberately, and by the time he was flat broke again, had jumped at the proposition presented so subtlety to him, and was ready to agree to the KGB proposals. He had fallen out of favour with his Royalist friends. Didn't they all act very superior towards him, anyway. To be handsomely paid, for doing what he had come to think were nationalistic reasons, was enough to persuade him that he was doing his duty to the mother country.

So, goes the reasoning of any spy, but the balance between patriotism and risk are always fluid, and the element of corruption, must never override the principles of valour, and in Georgiou's case, money was his overriding consideration.

He had been assigned to a very agreeable task as bodyguard to one of his diplomatic contacts in the Naval Division and was very happy with his job. The fact was, he was doing rather well, in another department of his life. He felt he had really 'won the candy' as the girls around his boss were very willing to take him as a substitute sometimes.

His prowess with the ladies increased as he was taught all the tricks they peddled, always letting him think he was in control, but he was a very eager pupil and his appetite just got bigger.

He had been angry on Friday evening to have had one of his amorous encounters discovered. His guard dog had alerted him to an intruder only to find a more serious situation develop. He then had to answer to his boss as to how the dog had been killed, and all that uncovered his dalliances.

So, he was not in a good frame of mind to be instructed on his duties for next week at the Bastille Day Celebrations. He had been given a list of Russian Emigrés and he was startled to find the name Stefan Baronski amongst the guests and wondered who he was.

Hadn't the mock heist of last Xmas been something to do with him? He paused, looking down the list, and began to question his assumption that Nicholas was the dead body washed up downstream of their rendezvous point.

Could Nicholas really have survived in those wintry waters? What temperature would it have been? (Could he have anticipated the evening events which had resulted in the death of Boris at the Arts Ball) and had some back up plan? His fevered imagination found many different ways that he may have been fooled, and cursed as he accepted it was possible. He had a score to settle there if ever he met up with Nicholas.

****

Minka and Tasha were delighted to have the opportunity to take Stefan, that famous Russian dissident, well known for his fight against tyranny, to be among them to meet his fellow emigrés. They were all looking forward to the event.

Nicholas had contacted them earlier in the week to check on his father's progress but they had not been able to contact him since. They had also checked with Alex as to his attendance and all they wished for now, was a continuation of the lovely hot weather.

For ten years they had acted as guardians to Nicholas. The return of his real father Stefan had left them slightly bereft, in their new role of godparents. Tasha particularly, did not quite know what his new status would involve. They had happily taken Nicholas into their home when they had seen this to be a debt of honour, to Stefan for saving Tasha from drowning in the wartime sinking of his ship. Now his real father had returned, Tasha began to wonder what his future position would be, but hoped he would be seen as a wise councilor.

Minka, at least, would not change her motherly role as she would always treat Nicholas as one of the family, and it seemed that she had just added his father Stefan to her responsibilities, for he appeared to her, in the role of a wayward child.

They were happy to be taking Stefan to the celebrations but wondered whether he was wise to choose

such a public arena. It would draw attention to things best left obscure, and Nicholas had carved a new persona out of his old one. Most people would not recognize him from the boy he was, from the man he now had become. There were some who bore him ill will, if his real role was known.

In particular, Tasha knew that Georgiou had ranted and raved about Nicholas and he wondered at what level they had been involved. He was a nasty piece of work who, it now transpired, was a son of an official of the new order in Russia, and his instincts told Tasha that he was not to be trusted. Georgiou was far too self-serving and no reports he had of him were ever complimentary. His womanising, gambling and contacts with underworld low life thugs at his East End boxing club, had appalled most of his erstwhile friends in Kensington, and only his father's position, gave him any credence in their society.

When Tasha pondered this, he felt he must warn Nicholas of this enmity from Georgiou, so that he could be on his guard. He decided to have a word with Alex to watch Nicholas' back. There were so many different groupings, unfolding at the event, that he feared it was becoming an explosive mix.

Perhaps it was time to talk to Sir Charles to seek his perspective.

****

Sir Charles was cross, as events were not going well. Much that he had heard during the past week, had been bad, and the potential for things to get even worse, was dawning on him. He called Ian Duncan into the office and gave him the up-to-date information on events.

"It looks very likely that we have a massive breach in security and we must get positive proof of this. We can't take this to the Prime Minister unless we are absolutely sure of our facts, but the evidence is beginning to be very damning. The question is, what do we advise him to do about it?"

They spent the morning analysing the implications and advice they should recommend to the P.M.

Their transatlantic associates in the CIA would be furious at any breach in security and would be paranoid about any fall-out in their direction. They looked as if they had troubles of their own, with the Castro Government in Cuba, expelling so many people, many of whom, had eventually found their way to the coast of Florida. They certainly didn't want any other agitations and provocations with a Communist State. After all, they had not come out of their involvement with the ex-government of Cuba in the Spring, to want another disturbance so soon.

"Well Ian you have been very clear headed in your appraisal of the situation and I am pleased with your progress. You are very good at analysis. How do you think you are coming on with intuition, empathy and imagination?" He asked in his role as master.

"Well to tell you the truth, Sir, I don't think that I am quite as certain of my ground there."

"Aha, yes. How did you get on with your date last week?" He asked.

Ian looked abashed at this enquiry. "Well, I was glad to get it over with in the end." And he recounted Carole's reaction to the film. "I thought that it would be a really hot date, but we didn't seem to have anything in common. Her reaction to the film was totally dramatic."

Sir Charles leant back and looked at the young man for a minute and recognised his own faults laid out in front of him. It had been a hard road for him to travel, to understand other's reactions and how these could be manipulated to serve his purpose. Here was a young man who had many qualifications, but who struggled with the same difficulties of empathy, as he himself had once done.

After a minute, he said. "You have read Carole's 'profile' haven't you? Why do you think she reacted like that?"

Ian shook his head. It had only been an over dramatic version of Romeo and Juliet and she had taken it all so much to heart.

He looked enquiringly at his boss.

Patiently Sir Charles asked. "What connections to real life did you see?"

Ian thought and said in student speak. "Well, it was a polemic of the great American racial interactions."

"And what do you think she saw in it? Think carefully now." Asked Sir Charles.

Ian looked at Sir Charles and hoped he would give some inkling of the answer.

"Well, I supposed the same as me, but she bloody well didn't." He said explosively as he remembered her embarrassing tears.

Sir Charles leant back again and sighed, yes, this man would end up, as he had ended up, behind a desk, pulling the strings, and moving the pieces. His lack of human connection would forever force him to stand aloof from real emotion.

That Carole had cried because she had felt the loss of her lover and couldn't see any future for them, was completely lost on the young man. Yes, he would be able to move the pieces but he would not be able to feel the breeze as they passed by.

Yet it was written there in her profile if Ian had intuition to see.

CHAPTER 16

Delirium

Carole was growing concerned about Nicholas as he seemed to have taken fever from his wound and she did not know what her course of action should be. She knew he needed to get to hospital but if she could provide him with a course of antibiotics, without questions being asked, it would be better for everybody: It would be very awkward to break off their investigations.

She soaked a cloth in cold water and sponged his face and shoulders but hesitated to go further and disturb the surface of the wound. It had turned red and swollen and there was heat emanating from the area, but otherwise was not looking ugly.

She knew that she could ring for back up but was anxious that Nicholas would hate this fuss. She remembered how Ian had hated fuss but she thought she could trust him to be dispassionate about this and could be relied upon just to do as she asked him to do.

Two hours later Ian arrived at the boat with the package of antibiotics. He checked Nicholas over and examined the wounds with a professional eye.

"That is a deep wound he has sustained but it is not too raw. I don't like the fever but I think the antibiotics will help control that."

He examined the man on the bunk once more and looked back at Carole standing there with no hysterics but an anxious look on her face.

He remembered the question that Sir Charles had posed him earlier and he finally got the point of it. Yes, here was the man she had lost and this time he understood her fear.

"I think it would be a good idea if I stayed overnight. If we are lucky, his fever will break in by then, but if not then we have to arrange a discreet ambulance."

She nodded her gratitude but refrained from any histrionics.

"We'll take turns watching him but keep the cold compress and bathing going to help keep the temperature under control. He touched her hand tentatively and said. And a good cup of tea and a bite to eat might be a good idea."

She focused her gaze on him and realised he had talents she had overlooked and she forgave him his crassness of the other evening.

She handed him a mug and offered a bowl of

cornflakes. "I'm afraid that's all I can offer you. I have been too busy to leave the boat for any food."

"That's fine by me. He smiled. But how about I get some fish and chips later. I passed a shop not far away. It is going to be a long night."

Her stomach heaved with anxiety, too stressed to care that she had not eaten yet today and that what he had said made sense. They should also think of something for Nicholas for when he awoke.

Ian made a schedule to take turns at watching and she put his kitbag into the aft cabin. If he had not guessed their relationship he knew it now for she hadn't been sleeping in the aft cabin.

In the moments between the changeover of their watch, she gave him a report of their night activities upriver at Basildon and he nodded in confirmation of what he already knew.

When Ian finally went to fetch some fish and chips and they were sitting eating them, she asked him how he knew so much about medicine.

Ian explained that he had trained as a doctor but had found the emotional side too difficult to handle. He found the puzzles he had to solve now, much easier than dealing with emotional relatives.

When Ian finished his watch at 3.00 a.m. he checked

Nicholas again and grunted in satisfaction. He could see that he was sleeping easily and the fever had broken. He went to tell her the news but saw that she was fast asleep and he left her to finish the night and tiptoed back beside Nicholas. Was Nicholas going to get a surprise in the morning, he thought, and a smile crossed his face.

Nicholas woke to a loud snoring and was disorientated by finding a young man on the bunk opposite. Had Carole turned into a troll as he saw the face opposite, with mouth wide open omitting such a horrible noise? He tried to rise and pain shot through his arm. He remembered some of the events of the night and was conscious of conversations in the background.

Where was Carole, he thought, as his brain clicked into gear? He crawled out of his bunk and used the heads, conscious of the urgent prompting of his bladder. He sat there and let bodily relief bring his brain back to full throttle.

He remembered the dog that had leapt at him, just as he thought that he was home and dry, and the bite to his arm that the dog had given, as the animal had almost overwhelmed him. He had just been able to land a knife blow before he had sustained further damage.

He had seen the party in full swing and the erotic nature of much of it. He had recognized several people in compromising positions but saw no obvious breach of security. He had just decided to leave when he was surprised, out in the limousine in the driveway, to come upon another writhing couple and was shocked to find that it was Georgiou. He stepped back out of sight and hightailed it back down the lawn to the river below.

Here at last was a chink of evidence and, in his haste to get back to the boat, he had alerted that brute of an Alsatian who had done him this harm. He ruefully acknowledged the momentary lapse in caution but knew that a vital link might have been found. Georgiou, he now knew, was the son of Russian Embassy staff.

The disturbance had brought Ian out of his sleep and as Nicholas returned to the cabin he looked at the awakened man and said aggressively. "Who the hell are you? What are you doing here and what in thunder have you done to my wife?" Maintaining his cover story, he had used this title as he feared some game was being played by opposing interest.

"OK, old man, don't get yourself agitated. The stranger drawled. "You're hardly in a fit state for that, are you?" The fierce look had gone from Nicholas's face but the tension in his body didn't lessen.

"Actually." the stranger continued. "I'm your Guardian Angel and Carole is sleeping off her vigil. We have been rather anxious about you!' That was a bit of a nasty bite you sustained in your nighttime perambulations and not giving it immediate attention, rather let it fester a bit. In fact, you had us both worried there." He paused. "I'm Ian by the way." And he held out his hand to shake hands in formal greeting. Nicholas hesitated then responded in kind.

"Well Ian, how do you fit into the picture? Why did Carole call you?"

Ian proceeded to explain. "Well, she and I are to be bound together later in the month and she rather thought I should be brought into the picture."

Nicholas couldn't believe what he was hearing. His heart sank, as he misinterpreted what Ian was saying.

'What?" He faltered. "What do you mean, 'bound together'. Are you to be married?"

"No, no, good Lord, no." Ian hastily assured him and Nicholas sat down suddenly as he was feeling rather faint. "I didn't mean that at all but I have to be careful what I say! You must realise that I am also one of Sir Charles's protégées."

He looked at his patient's pallor and decided that explanations could keep.

He said hastily. "Look, there's plenty of time for catching up, but it is time you had some food inside you. Rest there, and I will get you some cornflakes." And he turned to the galley and left Nicholas already lying on the bunk. He put the kettle on quietly and wondered whether to continue or slip into the awakening town for rather more provisions.

He moved quietly across to the aft cabin but Carole

had not been disturbed by their conversation and he returned to the galley turned off the heat and stepped ashore.

He realised, that perhaps Carole should find Nicholas recovering without his presence. He thought of Sir Charles and laughed softly as he made his way up Castle Street to find food.

"I think he would be proud of me this morning." Ian thought as he grasped the kernel of the situation, and did not hurry back too soon.

The sound of quickening noises outside the boat had eventually woken Carole who immediately thought about their patient. She threw on her jumper over pyjamas and looked out onto the world. The sky was leaden with threatening rain clouds scudding across from the west. She shivered at the sudden change in temperature from her cabin, then tiptoed into the galley and through into the fore cabin looking anxiously at Nicholas.

There was no sign of Ian, but all was peaceful on the bunk beside her. There was no sign of the fever that had wracked Nicholas, and his steady breathing told her all was well. She gazed down at him in relief and couldn't restrain from kissing the hand below the bandage and holding it to her breast. The sleeping man stirred but did not wake as she knelt there holding his hand.

Some minutes later her cramped limbs were forced to adjust and this time the sleeping man stirred. He lay there with his hand warm in hers, and held the precious moment. Where was that fellow, what did he say his name was, another Alex, Alistair, Ian, yes that was it? He feigned sleep for a minute more, but did not sense or hear his rival!

"Carole, Carole." He whispered and, as she leant to hear, he put his good arm over onto her hair and stroked it. She turned her head and kissed him on the lips.

He realised in that moment that his energy was returning to him as he drew her close but she resisted with a relieved laugh.

"Lordy master." She said in mock submission. "You's far too ill to think of do's capers!" And he relinquished his hold, satisfied that there would be time enough later.

She went through to the galley and mixed Ovaltine and plenty of sugar into two cups and brought them through to him.

"Here you are, drink this, you need some quick energy if we are to restore you to health. That's all I can rustle up but I guess Ian has gone for some provisions. We had meant to get stocked up last night but left it too late in the end.

"Ah. He said slowly, Ian?" And waited for some reaction in her face.

"Yes, Ian. He is my escort for the celebrations next Saturday." She hesitated as she realised the height of his interest.

"I called upon his help as I didn't think that hospital was appropriate. I thought that if he could procure some antibiotics, we could manage things between us, so to speak." And she looked coyly at his thunderous expression.

She stopped her teasing as she was aware that his reaction had sent a delicious frisson of power through her. "Actually, I couldn't have managed without him." She said in a sober voice looking at him steadily again. "We took turns on patient-watch, all day and night, and he was ready to call in reinforcement if necessary. So, I'm indebted to him for keeping you alive, because, what would I have done if I lost you again." And he was satisfied at the place he held in her affections.

Just then, they heard a heavy clatter of feet on the pontoon and Ian hailed them loudly. "Breakfast you two, the grocer has arrived."

He produced his bounty and proceeded to empty his shopping bag. "Now let me see."

"Ian that's a massive amount of food" Carole protested.

"Oh, do you think so?" He said as he looked doubtfully at the smoked haddock, eggs, bread, milk, sausages, bacon and black pudding. "Well I don't think so, you are cooking for healthy men here and a Scot to boot. I am sure you agree, don't you Nicholas?" And as they eyed each other over the black pudding they cemented a friendship of mutual respect.

"I hope that includes a good dram of whisky in there too?" Nicholas said feebly, and with a sailor's salute Ian gaily produced a bottle of that noble nectar. "You bet, Sir!"

They set to, happily preparing the selection of odd provisions. She was perplexed as to how she should cook all these things together, in one pan, but with Ian's guidance, they soon had a hearty meal.

The clouds had cleared slightly, so they took it all out into the cockpit.

Nicholas was looking slightly better now and his random instructions about proceedings in the galley, boded well for his recovery. Exasperated, Carole finally banished him to the cockpit to check up on all things 'boaty.'

Half an hour later the gaping hole in his stomach was treated to an exotic mixture of haddock, poached egg, bacon, sausages, black pudding, tomatoes and fried bread.

They ate in complete silence and when the tea was poured, Ian brought out the whisky. Nicholas nodded blissfully and decided, there and then, that he wanted to go sailing with this companion. The fraternity of seagoing friends was a bond for life, as they each recognised in the other, someone they could trust if things got rough.

Within an hour Nicholas was beginning to feel a return in strength. He knew he was still weak but the restorative powers of a fit man didn't usually take long to activate. While they had been eating, the delicious smells from open air eating, had attracted some attention from the passing strollers on the riverside quay. It had originally been Nicholas' intention to dock here to blend in with the other river users. But their stay had been long enough to attract attention from their boating neighbours, when jocular banter was shot at them about their lovely breakfast. Boating folk were essentially friendly, but their natural curiosity could recall many details of different boats and they liked to talk over the finer details of their crafts. It would not do to let them get too curious, as there was a large discrepancy between boat and engine, which would be immediately apparent to a more observant boat owner.

They decided that Ian should stay with them for the day as an honoured guest, and to give more cover to their being holiday makers. They would leave when the boat owners went quayside for their evening meal. The Saturday changeover of boat hirers for some of the crafts, might also mask their own departure.

They still had some time to kill and so, with rain starting, they went inside the cabin to bring Ian up to date with the situation, and his face became grave.

"Damn and hellfire." He said untypically agitated. "This is all we need. A confirmation of all we suspected. But it's not quite enough, is it?"

"No." Agreed Nicholas "But I think next week's celebrations might throw up some clinchers."

Ian said anxiously. "We can't afford to let this develop too long. We don't know how much secret information has been lost already. Well yes, we hope next weekend might produce some evidence, but in the meantime, go about your business as you were, and hope that we have a stroke of luck."

They shelved their worries and talked about boats and engines and fast cars, which were all fascinating to young men, but they refrained from mentioning fast women, in their idle chatter, deeming it was inappropriate, but Carole knew that was the missing element to their male anecdotes!

She allowed the conversation to drift past her and soon was fast asleep. After the strain of the last 24 hours, she was in need of sleep and the two men kept watch over her.

CHAPTER 17

The Watcher over the River

They decided that a turn of the town would do them all good and they walked up arm-in-arm until they found a tearoom in the high street. It had rained whilst they had been in the cabin and the streets were wet but the brightness of the sun made them sparkle. They climbed up to the castle and admired its battlements, a bastion of mediaeval armaments and guards stood at its main gates. They walked towards the Town Hall and quickly found Ye Olde Tea Shoppe opposite.

They tucked themselves at the back of the room, as they joined all the drenched holidaymakers clutching at some cheerfulness, out of the rain. For them, the rain had no importance, but the cakes piled high on the counter held great promise. They ordered Welsh rarebit and beans on toast with extra white sliced bread. They were unable to make an instant decision on the cakes, so had a cake stand put in the middle of the table to tempt them later. By this time, Carole was defeated but the two men just went on eating as though they had never eaten at all that day!

They parted company with Ian, who had to return

home, and turning, at a leisurely pace towards Eton and the river, admired the school like all the other tourists.

She questioned him about his own school life and he staunchly defended his own public school on the River Itchen at Winchester.

"You do all stick together, don't you?" She remarked idly.

"Well, of course, it was my home for so many years and loyalties count, don't you think?"

"Yes," she said thoughtfully, "but my loyalties seem to spring from a place, an anchoring into the soil of England."

"I know what you mean. For many years my anchorage, was my memory of the Caucasus and the feeling of the land, and going to Winchester gave me something of that feeling again."

"Is it enough to have that sense about a school, as it is to have the same loyalty to Queen and Country?" She questioned him seriously. For a long few minutes he was silent.

"Yes, I think it is, but it is also the attachments you make to the people to the people you love...he paused again. "I had thought that was enough – indeed, I was sure, but recently I had cause to long for a deeper commitment to this land, to its farms and rivers, and people and my old memories of childhood awakened in me, a need to become part of this land, to this countryside, to a village of my choosing that I could really call home."

He turned to her and she gave him a loving look. Oh, so near, he thought, so near, but not yet. They had work to do and he must hold back from telling her of his dreams of Shakespeare Country!

He broke himself free from her gaze and shook her slightly. "Come on," he said, "we've work to do. Let's get started before that next black cloud overtakes us." He took her hand in his and pulled her gently and they raced down the hill back to their haven, the perfect expression of young lovers on a Sunday afternoon.

People smiled as they watched their flight but there was one watcher who didn't smile and who looked in puzzlement at the couple. There was something familiar about them both. He couldn't quite recall who they were, but he had the distinct feeling that he knew them.

CHAPTER 18

More News of Foreboding

They arrived at the quay just as the clouds clashed and thundered overhead. Streaks of lightning lit up the late afternoon sky and there was nothing for it, but to batten themselves down in the cabin. They had planned to leave at about 7.00 p.m. and make it to Cookham by late evening whilst there was still enough river traffic for them to blend in.

Nicholas looked at Carole and she blushed, suddenly shy of her thoughts and longings, but all she really wanted was to hold him in her arms. Her passion was abated for the time being, but she had great need of his presence. He knew intuitively that this was a moment to savour and reached his arms to her. Their kiss expressed all the love and longing that their earlier passion had not and he was in no hurry to force their union.

The lightning flashed and the thunder rumbled but inside the cabin, all was calm. They instinctively knew that this was a very special moment, where love and not lust held sway, and they understood the relationship between the two passions.

In their work, they were about to enter a world of pure lust, and it was good that they could tell the difference between those two elements.

****

After a night of storms, they had lain in each other's arms and the anxiety of her vigil and the pain of his arm had settled their night-time activities but the morning brought sunshine and a return of passion and Carole teased and coaxed a stirring in him and did her best to leave his arm unsullied by their gyrations.

They slipped their mooring and headed upstream due west until they reached where the river gradually turned north on its way to Cookham. The river was full of craft but most, now seemed to be moving purposefully to their assorted destinations.

Later that morning they had reached Runnymede and anchored up by the field made famous for its seal upon English laws, made by English nobles against the tyranny of a French born Englishman. They had given that Burgundian Prince, King John, an ultimatum, and the English Parliament, under the Seal of the Magna Carta, had been born. Their interest in this monument was quickened by Nicholas's knowledge of his birth country's rebellion against absolute rule and he thought this English agreement with their king had been an altogether better outcome than his country, Russia, had experienced.

"Oh, don't be too sure of that." Said Carole. "We managed to cut off the head of a few more kings and queens before we settled for what we call democracy." And they laughed happily. They were very conscious of their part present task of trying to keeping Britain stable, and these monuments to the past did not seem remote at all. There were always threats, by powerful forces, from time to time, to the good governance of a country, and they had signed up to maintain the 'status quo'.

She had asked Nicholas to take her to Cookham church, as she had seen many of Stanley Spencer's paintings. She said they were a typical illustration of country people and he recognised their portraits as the faces of country folk everywhere, slightly bovine and stoic, but he loved every one of them.

They walked the fields around the village and stopped for lunch back at the Coach and Horses. The steps they took together, in these fields and villages of England, helped bind him to her earth, her fields and sky, and the peeling of the bells of every village church, made him more aware of the wonderful land of his adoption. Through her, he knew that he must completely commit to this country's defense. His response to Sir Charles's call had been lukewarm, tinged with loyalty and revulsion at the Soviet treatment of his father, but now, he was seeing this country through his lover's eyes, and marking what was good about it.

Of course, he was not blinded to its faults, and its autocratic approach to trade was the hangover from the

Empire. It seemed to Nicholas that they had managed its dismantlement rather well. The people of those countries, even preferred to come here to live, after all, and fundamentally it had given him refuge also, in time of need, and that required him to honour this land and its people.

Days and nights passed in loving and looking and evenings, listening and searching, eager to hear some snippet of information about the house they had come to watch.

By Thursday, they had not traced any bit of news of Basildon, until they returned to the Coach and Horses at Maidenhead and, once again, there was a group of men at the bar. Nicholas spotted a couple of them that he recognised from the previous week, who again were some of the noisiest of the group.

Nicholas and Carole sat with their backs to the bar, overlooking the river, and again ate steak and chips and a wonderful summer pudding. They were happy to sample the beer, although most of those on offer were lead breweries. At the Bar, they spotted a Fullers beer and ordered some London Pride.

Carole spoke up warmly about cider, especially the variety they brewed at home, and he absentmindedly agreed, with feeling that it was, but would not be drawn on his acquaintance with that brew. He laughed and shook his head and teased her with his air of mystery.

Over at the Bar, the talk was getting louder and Nicholas became more attentive to their talk. "They certainly don't like snoopers when they have certain VIPs to their gatherings. Georgy was in here on Saturday night, hopping mad. You know Georgy, he's the one with boxing friends who's handy with his fists in any argument. Anyway, he was in here earlier, as I say, and he was in a real ugly mood. Swore he would get even with an intruder who killed his dog."

"Oh, you know Georgy, he's all talk!" Said another scornfully.

Whilst this conversation was going on Nicholas had gone to the bar to pay his bill and heard another man say. "Oh, I don't know, he's certainly not all talk when it comes to the ladies, reckons they are queueing up for him. He's quite an athlete there, old sport, I know because." The talk got coarser and more private and there was a loud burst of laughter from the group.

"Well as I was saying," said the first man, "he came in here again on Monday, and he was real mean. He had calmed down but he looked like a man possessed and was saying he reckoned he knew who it was that had killed his dog and he was out to get him. Georgiou said, 'the man couldn't hide as he was the man with the blue eyes'." As the speaker said that, the bartender was just handing Nicholas his change and their eyes met, locking for a split second.

He turned to leave the bar fully aware that the man had registered him. He whispered to Carole that they must remain calm but to move out of the pub rather quietly.

The landlord was looking very speculatively over at their table but decided not to say anything. He didn't want any trouble and the young buck they were talking about, was a mean character. It looked to him that the man by the window, with that lovely young lady, deserved a bit of a break. He had already defined them as beauty and the beast but he felt tonight, that the man was more of a wounded animal than a monster, and he remained silent.

CHAPTER 19

The Idyll Ends

They walked quickly to the pontoon and jumped on to the boat. Nicholas had instructed Carole to be ready to cast off as they were moving.

She felt his concern and fell in with his instructions, without asking questions.

How the devil had his enemy tracked him down and why did Georgiou think that he was responsible for the dog's death? Nicholas could only surmise that they had been spotted somewhere on the river and cursed under his breath.

They would have to put some miles between them and hope for some luck at the celebrations. He opened up the throttle and they sped as fast as conditions allowed. They anchored up above the first lock they came to and waited for morning.

Nicholas remembered that he had not checked in with his father since before the dog bite, and needed to reassure himself of his father's welfare.

He slept fitfully that night thinking of the implications of Georgiou's discovery. He had thought that his altered appearance would be a sufficient disguise but he now realised he had a fatal distinguishing feature – his eyes. He had thought that his father's decision to come to the Party had laid down a gauntlet to the KGB, who might take unkindly to Stefan's reappearance in another country, especially if he became an active dissident writer again.

Nicholas had assumed that he would lead a quiet life in the country with his father, but he would not dissuade his father from his chosen path. That meant that Nicholas was more exposed than he had anticipated, to the vindictiveness of Georgiou, and he was at a loss as to how he could defend himself, if Georgiou really wanted blood.

Carole responded to his early morning wake up and they sped towards the lock. The lockkeeper was surprised at their early arrival but was in no hurry. They waited impatiently for him to fill the lock and did not engage in their usual banter. They had many locks and many miles to cover before nightfall.

She had been aware that Nicholas had been troubled about something ever since they had left the pub and, his focused actions since, made her sense that this was serious business they had been engaged upon. All week she had been in their special bubble, and last night it burst, and brought her back to the reality of their mission. That he had heard something she guessed, but he was not disclosing his findings.

She followed his orders and did not trouble him

further with questions as they headed downstream.

****

Georgiou was finding the world, was not to his liking. The job as bodyguard to the Naval Attaché was under threat. He was asked to account for his movements before the dog was killed, and found it hard to explain his absence. His amorous encounter was also exposed and altogether his position was under review.

He had been fond of the dog and raged and cursed at the intruder for such an act. Georgiou vowed he would get even, and had become convinced with whom he was dealing.

He had gone to Windsor afterwards to see one of his racing friends, who had been at Eton, and chance had taken him to the river that day and up towards the school. He had not, at first, been able to recognise Carole and Nicholas. There was something familiar about this couple, so obviously in love, but later thought of Carole, and the association made him believe it was Nicholas, despite his face-altering scar and beard, and grey streaked hair. That he was much altered had confused Georgiou, but there was sufficient about his movements and physique to make a connection.

He was a man with fixed obsessions and Nicholas was one of them. He could not see his supposedly dead friend, without jumping to conclusions and in this instance, he was right. All Nicholas' careful plans to disguise himself at the Bastille Day party, were blown out of the water by this man's hunter instincts. He had the perfect qualifications to make a good spy, being able to make those leaps of intuition.

He railed at his misfortune for four whole days but began to see a way to hurt Nicholas that had more than a touch of poetic justice to it. He would combine his natural predeliction, with wounding Nicholas where it would hurt most and his 'chippy' bounce came back to him.

He began to look forward to the celebrations that he was to attend on Saturday and his surly demeanour, changed to ingratiating willingness to please. In the meantime, things were looking brighter for him, if his plan worked, and he was more than willing to make himself useful.

The Event, promised to be very much to his liking, as there would be many lovely ladies there, and he didn't usually have any trouble in that direction. He dismissed from mind his unfortunate lapse, and planned his 'coup de grace'.

****

Sir Charles was beginning to have some anxiety about his plans. He knew that, slight though it was, Nicholas's information began to give credence to his fears of a lapse in security, through the oldest profession in the world. If the suspects had indeed been sharing lovers, then the consequences were grave. Pillow talk was a very effective way to transfer useful information, after all he had used it himself with Carole and Nicholas at Christmas, and it even provided the opportunity to steal documents if anyone was silly enough to leave them around.

He hoped that this had not happened but the signs were full of foreboding.

He was also cross at the news received from Commander Counter about Stefan Baronski's return to public life. It would inevitably, expose Nicholas to some form of reprisal, for his part in rescuing his father, and the KGB would be alerted to that fact.

He was reassured that Ian would be good back up. He had a clear head and would provide cover for Carole. He was not so sure about what he could do to help Nicholas as his role was to be a 'lure for his bird' and was already prepared for that role.

He decided to call upon his contacts in the River Police patrol. They had been useful in the past and he remembered that two of them would suit his purpose admirably. They had been very handy in the 'Pearls Affair' and would have no difficulty in spotting where the danger would come from.

Georgiou might have thought it wise to lie low in a police cell last autumn, but it had the disadvantage of more firmly fixing his face and character, onto the memory of the officers in charge and that had decided advantages when Sir Charles needed back up for his plan.

****

Carol and Nicholas travelled purposefully down river and made progress to Kingston-on-Thames. They had stopped briefly at Richmond for Nicholas to contact Sir Charles and his father. He was relieved to hear Stefan on the line, with a voice much stronger and positive and he was glad that he was enjoying the visit to his old friends. He needed to warn his father that they could not acknowledge each other at the celebrations, but explained no more. This alarmed his father. Nicholas knew that if he was to greet his family, the success of his disguise, would be compromised.

Next, he rang Sir Charles with more information of last night's conversations and suggested that, an independent witness to events might be forthcoming, from the landlord of the Coach and Horses, who seemed to know when to keep quiet. He understood that the landlord could have raised speculation with the men at the bar if he had so wished. The landlord had definitely registered Nicholas' blue eyes but had not shown any reaction.

The role of the landlord had many of the qualities of his profession, and he could be relied upon to be 'a wise monkey!'

Final preparations and plans were arranged for tomorrow and he returned to the boat well satisfied, that he had done all he could to anticipate anything unexpected.

****

He returned to the boat with a grin on his face, like any sportsman anticipating a match beforehand and Carole could see the change in him. His natural charm and bonhomie had reasserted itself. He stepped on board and gave her a big hug, lightly kissing her on her lips. He handed her a bag of food and a bottle of wine. "The chase is on." He whispered as she realised that his words held more than one meaning and they fenced and flirted with each other all down the river till sunset.

They moored up on the backside of an eyot near Kingston-upon-Thames out of sight of most of the river traffic. The sunny weather had reasserted its dominance, after the storms of yesterday and all the bankside of their island retreat bustled with life.

The smell of food cooking had brought them an army of friends looking for tit bits. A mother coot with her string of chicks waddled past pecking the side of the boat as if to say 'hey, what about us?' Next there were ducks coming to look at them and assert their requests and they took delight in all the sights and sounds around them. The slight breeze that had sprung up had kept the gnats and midges at bay and prolonged their enjoyment of the riverside sunset. As dusk came, a water vole busied itself along the reeds in the banks. It scurried along a small sandbank opposite the island and looked at them enquiringly. He was used to their kind invading his territory but, other than that cursory look, took himself busily up the river.

All around them the sounds of roosting birdsong whistled and trilled and the dance of the starlings traced a musical score in the pink and purple sky. Swans and ducks flew their military formations, flying who knew where, to their evening fastness.

It seemed to Nicholas that the panoply of life on that magical evening, was saying to them. "Here I am, this is the country and river and stream that you must love if you are to understand your inheritance: guard it well."

Their loving that night seemed to encompass that commitment and there was no haste in their actions and when finally, their crest was reached, there was complete surrender and they knew that this love was forever.

CHAPTER 20

Robespierre

Nicholas woke to the same sounds of the evening before, birdsong and bustle and the awakening sun, heralded a fine day for the Party.

Turning to the woman breathing softly beside him, he was in no hurry to awaken this sleeping beauty as he knew later, they would need their wits about them. He was content to gaze adoringly at, her brow, her closed eyelids, her retroussé nose and full sweetheart rosy lips swollen still from the emotion of their night time loving and he longed to kiss her again and awaken their moments of passion. But, the preparations for the day had reasserted themselves, and he had to remain content with these precious moments, before the world claimed them.

Sometime later he heard the striking of a church clock across the water, and prepared for the day ahead.

****

They had arranged to meet Ian at a small discreet hotel at Hampton Wick, where they could properly prepare for the Party. He was to bring their clothes from London and the necessary items that Nicholas had requested. They all looked spruce and dandy in their summer finery. The men were requested to wear either something formal, Ian was dressed in a DJ, and Carole had a short white dress and Cuban heeled shoes. No point in wearing her stilettos here, she thought, her shoes would be off her feet before they had taken two steps on that soft manicured lawn. The lovely sun-kissed arms and long legs, that she had displayed to advantage in brief shorts during the past week, contrasted the white of her simple dress. The glow of her loving was still upon her and Ian could fully appreciate the stunning affect. He sighed, only for one day. He thought of Nicholas. Lucky chap, but she's mine for just one day. Then he remembered her emotional outburst at 'West Side Story,' and left any regrets behind, knowing he could never handle the emotional outbursts she had exhibited.

Meanwhile Nicholas was donning his fancy dress costume as Robespierre, be- wigged and bespectacled. He had taken the extra precaution of wearing coloured contact lenses to confuse Georgiou or any other prying eyes, and he presented himself to them both.

"My, you do look fine." Said Carole in mock Southern belle voice.

"You'll do." Said Ian after an altogether more serious appraisal of his colleague.

****

Nicholas had spotted a quiet haven for docking the

boat. He set everything in order and stepped lightly onto the bank and strolled upwards through the meadow to the entrance to Wimple House. Around him, many of the guests were arriving, and his appearance was not especially flamboyant, as he walked up the driveway, looking myopically for his ticket. His bumbling search was noted by the security staff, as they checked his credentials. "Mr. Barr guest" and ticked his name off the list.

Nearby another guard was also observing the arrival of the guests and ticking off his own list. So far, he had seen no one of particular interest to him, but there were many more to come.

At 2.30 p.m. he spotted Carole arrive with a tall gangly fellow who looked particularly well in his evening suit, but Georgiou didn't rate his staying power. Ian had the type of physique that belied its strength.

He looked tall and very awkward, and his native country of Scotland had bred many like him, with sturdy joints and strong hands, that had become mountaineers and explorers, and there was much latent strength below that suave exterior. His fiery red hair should have alerted Georgiou to the nature of his opponent, for his Scottish ancestors were famed as fierce warriors.

****

Carole and Ian entered the house whose grandeur was superficial, as it was faded and unkempt, but the festivities

138

and dancing buntings, distracted the eye from its damp stained walls and sun-bleached décor. The gardens of the site were presently used as a teaching establishment, but the house was separate from the College, which had left the Gothic structure substantially intact since any occupation, over fifty years before. It had been subject to the depredations of the passing decades, including war damage, but enough of its grandeur remained to be impressive.

They walked through into the long gallery and saw that it overlooked the gardens and beyond to the Thames.

The riverside garden was informal but decorated with bunting, in red white and blue, and people in Republican Costume or formal attire gathered and mingled in the sunlight. Trays of drinks were circulated and large trestle tables were arranged in French style to accommodate all the guests, with napiery and flowers, representing a typical wine gatherers mayoral street party. The event was already lively, with a French accordion player entertaining them. It was anticipated that the evening would end with a firework display over the river. They were all invited to disport themselves on the lawn until the main event and small canapés were being served.

Carole was wide- eyed at the atmosphere that had been created and could only imagine that the Oxford and Cambridge Summer Balls had a similar air, but this was 'oh, so French.' She had been very interested in the house itself and was intrigued to know more, but the day was not entirely hers to indulge.

She was standing next to Ian when a lady and two gentlemen, who were also admiring the house and pictures, approached her. They were in the long gallery and most of the guests were now in the garden. Ian nodded courteously to the taller of the two gentlemen whom Ian immediately recognized by his naval gait. As one sailor to another he had warmed to this bluff, no nonsense salty seadog.

"Allow me sir, to introduce you to my friend, Carole Penny. I think perhaps you may remember her flat-mate Janice, at our last meeting at Christmas."

"Ah yes, of course. Minka, do you remember Janice at Christmas? At the Soirée, I believe." Said Tasha Counter.

"Oh, of course, such a lovely girl and you, Indeed, my dear, are a vision of English beauty. So happy to meet you."

She stopped, almost spilling out all she already knew about the young woman in front of her. That she had been the flat-mate of Janice, and who had somehow given the pearls to Nicholas for his father's release. She knew this, unofficially, through her husband and, as she gazed at Carole, Minka hoped she guessed more. Putting aside that speculation, she most dearly wanted to hug the young woman and thank her for her part in 'the pearls affair,' events, but managed to remain silent.

"Perhaps I may also introduce someone very special

to us my dear, who has made sufficient recovery from past events to come today." They turned to a distinguished looking lean gentleman with silver hair but with a face ravished by suffering.

She came forward to greet him and was looked at by two bright blue eyes, the colour of moonlight. She felt herself blush in total confusion and didn't immediately know what to do. This could only be Nicholas' father! Minka continued. "Stefan, I especially believe you would like to meet this young lady as I remember you wanted to thank someone. May I introduce Stefan Baronski." She stepped aside and allowed Stefan to regard Carole properly. He came forward and took both her hands in his and, in Gallic fashion, kissed them both solemnly and then for good measure kissed them again on both her palms.

It was a special moment and Stefan was unable to express his thanks in any other way.

Carole had gone from astonishment to embarrassment, to heartfelt gladness, recognising the profoundness of his gesture. This must be the father that had been spoken of so affectionately during the past week.

Without thinking further, she immediately returned his greeting by placing her arms about him and said.

"I am so glad you are restored to health." She looked speculatively at Tasha and Minka.

"There is much I could say about my friend Janice, but I guess you know that already, and since I am certain I am among friends, I will say that your…your illness has been the cause of much anxiety to someone I hold dear." She held her head high, and in that moment made three anxious, sentimental, caring people, very happy.

They moved out of the house and into the sunlight and found a shady place in the garden and drew up some chairs. Now, a French brass band was playing and everyone seemed to be enjoying themselves.

Stefan seemed to be basking in all the fuss he was receiving, as many people came up to pay their respects, and Tasha introduced them one by one.

As they all sat down to the meal, Stefan said. "This is all very well but when am I going to see Nicholas?" He said rather querulously.

"Oh, I am sure you will see him soon but he has many duties before he can get away." Carole reassured him.

Ian looked over at Carole who had changed during the past hour into another motherly hen fussing around Stefan, and he was glad that things were settled in that direction. He also echoed the thoughts of the landlord and thought Nicholas 'deserved a break.'

After the meal, Ian stood up and extracted Carole from the company. "I think we must leave you for the moment but will see you soon. Goodbye for now." Then, he carried Carole off to observe events.

CHAPTER 21

Enthralment

They walked back across the lawns to the terrace and recognised Sir Charles, who indicated a little scene being acted out near the shrubbery, and she caught her breath. She turned away in total confusion unable to watch this so public exhibition of betrayal. Ian put his arm around her shoulder and shook it.

"Why hen, dinna take on so." He said, in broad Scots to cover his embarrassment at Nicholas's public display of affection. "You know it's all play acting, don't you?" He said earnestly to reassure her, but he had seen what she had seen. The total enthralment of the man by a practiced harlot.

****

Steven and Alan Southgate were happy to earn some overtime money by being co-opted to the Bastille Day 'bash,' and when they knew their task, they were more than happy to oblige. They had reacted with utter dislike to the man they had captured out on the river last Christmas, and their instincts told them they would see him again. His kind were always trouble, and their speculation seemed to be correct.

That he was out to get his partner in crime (if that is what it was) they didn't doubt, as his death had been faked, and they and their friends from Gravesend (ha, that was a sick joke) had pulled him out half dead, and secured him passage on a very dubious ship. All at the behest of Sir Charles Willingham Wright, Bart, QC and DSO, who was able to pull a lot of strings in his profession.

Now they had been patrolling the river most of the day and had been able to spot Carole fairly easily but were still searching for Georgiou. They were fairly sure they had spotted Nicholas from the description they had been given. Especially when he was brought to their attention by the public display of licentiousness he was exhibiting towards a dark-haired beauty, who, by all indications they could see, welcomed his attentions.

So far, they had not spotted Georgiou, and they decided to moor up and patrol the grounds.

****

She was beautiful. He thought, with her long brown hair falling softly over her shoulders. He had known other more beautiful dark beauties, but he recognised that her attraction came from something more earthy than mere looks. She looked into his eyes like a praying mantis and her touch had him caught in her spell. He was surprised at the

145

instant male reaction he had to the look and touch of her hand on his arm. Yes, here indeed, was a woman that would drive a man to madness and end his career in one glorious satiation of passion.

She stroked his arm absently but leant closer until her opium damask rose perfume, filled his nostrils. She stepped back towards the shrubbery and he meekly followed her lead. He didn't see the tall, distinguished gentleman striding towards him, but others did, and smiled at the altercation that might be about to occur.

From the terrace, Sir Charles watched the Minister stride across the grass. He had just observed to him how perfectly everything had been done and how lovely all the ladies looked in their gay summer attire.

"No wonder." He had said. "Why, that lovely lady over there has turned even the head of a revolutionary like Robespierre." Laughing affably at his companion.

His companion's gaze was directed to the edge of the shrubbery where Nicholas was holding check on his rising passion giving a full display of his attraction to this woman, to all who cared to look, and hoping that it had been well noted by all. Except Carole he fervently hoped, who mercifully had been nowhere to be seen at the beginning of these theatricals.

Ian, standing by a distinguished looking guest innocently overlooking the river, was just describing a

146

memorable cricket match that he had watched and was beginning to describe to his bored companion, his leg action at the crease, when out of the corner of his eye he spotted things kicking off and moved his position to directly turn his companion's gaze towards the other action taking place on the far lawn.

The fellow turned his eyes to the scene and, without a word, left Ian standing in apparent bemusement, and strode to the scene.

It was a 'toss up' who would reach Nicholas first, but it was obvious that the two men had the same intention of breaking up the liaison. They glared fiercely at each other as they drew near and had all the appearance of two cocks fighting over one hen.

"Oh darling, so sorry to leave you all this time, but I see that this gallant Frenchman has been amusing you." He said dismissively to Nicholas and taking her arm, turned her back to the entertainments. Meanwhile her other 'amour' came up, purple in the face, and frog marched her across the full width of the lawn. With open mouth, the other gentleman hurried after them and they all disappeared behind the front of the house, to the total amusement of the whole party, who were quite aware of the significance of the scene. Nicholas took his eyes away from the retreating figures and adjusted his glasses foppishly. He was disturbed at how easily a beautiful stranger could use her wiles on him. He had come prepared to stage just that scene in the garden but was ashamed of his complete surrender to her charms. He knew that he had been capable of answering her call and was deeply disturbed by his reaction.

He didn't see Carole watching the whole event from the top of the terrace and he walked swiftly to the river to compose his disordered thoughts. He knew that he had achieved what Sir Charles wanted of him and that the proof had been there for all to see. They had proved that both men thought that they had priority over her favours and had demonstrated to all, their overlordship. That should be enough for Sir Charles but it was not enough for Nicholas, as he cooled his desires and thought about his despicable reaction to her charms.

He couldn't have anticipated Carole's reaction. When she realised the authenticity of his 'acting', she just wanted to get away from the scene in front of her.

CHAPTER 22

The Trap is Sprung

By now the sun was beginning to set and more of the guests were gathering at the riverside. Carole turned to the sanctuary and quiet of the house, for she could not bear to watch further. She passed through the gallery and, as she stopped to look further at the ceiling of fan tracery, heard someone say.

"You like a bit of art, do you miss?" Said a cockney voice of one of the security staff nearby.

"Oh yes." She said politely.

"Of course." he said, "they don't show much of it to the public. The best bits 'is over thar'." He confided, "out of the public gaze." He winked affably and continued. "If you don't mind a bit of a scramble, I can show you some more, if you like?" And she nodded assent. She could see that the fireworks were not quite ready and thought that she would have enough time to see them and hide away to recover her composure.

"They don't put these on display. They are far too precious." As she followed through one door into a vestibule and on through another into a tabernacle type room. He followed her through the door in front of him and shut it firmly behind her.

Carole had steadied her distress at seeing Nicholas in the compromising position with their suspect, and had fled to the house to try to bring her thoughts to a more rational state. Taking the bait to visit the other paintings, seeing it as a way to order her thoughts, she heard the door shut. She expected to see that the guard was behind her but found herself alone. Not alarmed, she gave herself over to looking at the pictures on the wall.

At first, Carole was not particularly focused and it was some minutes before she saw that the subject matter was all of the same kind. The first few nubile naked ladies, passed her scrutiny as rather overblown beauties with teasing poses, but it was not long before it dawned on her, that it was a room full of erotica and her senses were immediately alert with distaste. As she went through into the next room, her way was barred by a face that she knew, with a lecherous grin, all over it.

***

Georgiou had been successful in placing Carole in the garden and his suspicions were confirmed when he had seen her in the company of the old man who could only be Nicholas's father, and thought he had only to wait there for him to discover Nicholas' whereabouts, but no one resembling him, came near. His impatience was building but he could not see his quarry anywhere.

His attention was caught by the scene by the shrubbery and saw that it was the dark- haired strumpet he had ferried his boss to see, over the last month. He could feel his manhood rising as he looked at her provocative wooing of the man dressed as Robespierre, damaged of face, and with thick glasses on his nose.

He had looked such a harmless 'erk' that he had failed to spot Nicholas behind the disguise. Now, he found something was falling into place. Surely, he was wrong? He had looked at every one of the visitors in the eye, but had only seen his quarry's father holding court on the far side of the garden. But he knew in his heart that he had found who he was looking for. Those that love deeply and those that hate deeply, weren't they the two sides to passion? As lovers know lovers, so enemies know their enemy and triumphantly he knew that his instincts were right.

His passions, already aroused by the beautiful bitch he saw in the arms of his enemy, he set his trap.

He went over to one of his fellow guards that had worked this trick before with some hapless dolly bird, and explained who he must select and watched while the plan unfolded.

Nicholas had finished his role in this charade but was

shaken at his reaction to her charms. Were men so primitive that they couldn't keep their animal instincts in check, even when they loved someone else so deeply? How could he say he loved Carole when his reactions had been so primaeval?

He went in search of Ian and Carole to clear his mind of his passionate encounter. He was feeling soiled and wished that his job was finished and that he could return to their idyll. He looked around to where his father and the Counters were waiting for the fireworks to start. His father was wrapped up in a blanket and seemed to be enjoying his day out, but Nicholas could not see anything of Carole. He spotted Ian beginning to look at his watch with a worried frown and his heart sank.

Where was Carole and why wasn't she with Ian? He hurried across the lawn and met Ian's worried look.

****

Sir Charles was very satisfied with his day's work but was very fearful of the consequence, but had done his best to orchestrate this result. He had proved that there was a definite relationship between the woman and the Russian Attaché and a relationship between her and the Minister.

He was the Grand Puppet Master and had pulled all the strings to prove the connection. Sir Charles was proud of his powers to manipulate events and if he thought of the lives of his puppets and his effect on them, he would say, the good of his country came first.

They had done good work here and only hoped that his plans would have prevented any leak of sensitive material. But that was still to be proved. He had done what he came to do and could relax and enjoy the fireworks.

CHAPTER 23
Revenge is Sweet

Carole looked at the man in the doorway and recognised Georgiou.

"Oh hello, it's Georgiou, isn't it? What brings you here? She said inanely, fighting a rising panic. I hadn't seen you earlier, how are you?" She babbled on while he remained silent, looking at her in a strange way. She stopped and then explained that she had come to the room by mistake and perhaps he could help, by directing her back to the garden.

He continued to look at her with a strange glint in his eyes.

"I suppose I could Carole but it'll cost you." He said.

She put an uncertain smile on her face and said jokingly. "That's not very gallant of you Georgiou." Trying to keep him talking and keeping the conversation light.

She was beginning to think that he was looking at her in rather an ugly way.

"Where's your boyfriend then?" He said in scornful tones. "Is he running after a more exotic beauty?"

She drew in a breath knowing he was playing with her. "Who do you mean, Ian?"

"Ian, my arse." He laughed. "That gawky weakling." He mocked, "I don't think he'll be much good to you darling. "Not much blood in his veins. No." He said intensely. "You, need someone with a love of the ladies, someone who knows how to give a woman a good time, if you know what I mean." He advanced towards her and stroked her cheek and clasped her hair tightly in his thick hands, twisting her down below his face.

"Oh Georgiou, you're hurting me, what is the matter; why are you being like this with me. We're friends aren't we." She tried to reason with him but could see that he had something ugly in mind. She needed to keep him talking to delay him, so that her absence would be missed.

"Oh yes, we're friends alright, just like your FRIEND Nicholas is my friend: friend enough to shop me to the police and get far away with my share of the money. He shouldn't do that to a friend, should he? It's not friendly at all."

"What's that to do with me?" She protested trying to remain calm and ignorant of any involvement with Nicholas.

She desperately hoped that he did not know any more of their relationship but his next words shattered her hope.

He tightened his hold on her hair and pressed her to her knees. "You lying bitch." He shouted. "What's it to do with you? Everything to do with you, you're his lover, aren't you? You knew about the pearls and now his crazy old father has appeared strangely, out of the blue. I wonder how that happened?" And he forced her still further until she was on the floor.

"I don't know what you mean." She whimpered, desperate to protect Nicholas' identity intact.

He lessened his grip slightly and flipped her over on her back, gripping her shoulders as well as her hair.

"You lying stupid cunt. How dare you take me for a fool? That piece of shit will soon be laid bare for his resistance to the KGB and I will have great pleasure in personally inflicting pain upon him. Don't you know I saw you together last weekend and you didn't look like strangers to me!"

She knew at last that her protests were in vain and that any struggling would be useless. With despair in her heart she knew that the odds were completely against her and her wits were all that might save her.

"Sure, he's my boyfriend but you don't think I would be with him if he hadn't some of the money left. She laughed scornfully. Look at the state of him." And laughed again. He paused in his obvious intent and lessened his grip on her hair. At that moment, he went to open his trousers and she knew it was her only chance.

She brought her left knee up sharply into his groin and right ball with as much force a she could muster and he loosened his grip and clutched his penis, groaning with the pain. She rolled to the left and landed him another new blow to his chin.

Unexpected as it was, he managed to grab hold of her again and, with a snarl said. "You, filthy whore, I'll make you pay for that." As he clung onto her legs imprisoning them whilst recovering from her blows. All in the room was quiet as the first of the fireworks flared into the sky.

****

Nicholas reached Ian's side and asked, with dread in his heart. "Where's Carole?"

"I don't know." Said Ian. "I was waiting for her to return from the Ladies Room but she seems to have disappeared. It's got to be 10 minutes since I saw her last and she knew that the fireworks were starting."

Nicholas shook Ian's shoulders and looked straight at the other man. "Did she see my charade out there?"

"Well, yes." Ian said, realising the implications.

"Look, we need to think. Which way would she go?"

"Towards the long gallery and right to the cloakroom. Ian replied.

Let's take that path and see if anyone has seen her. She is, after all, fairly memorable."

They retraced her possible path and came to the long gallery. Here there was a security guard who appeared to be hanging around, neither watching the fireworks and not especially directing people.

"Excuse me," said Nicholas, "have you seen a young blonde lady come this way?"

"Who wants to know?" He prevaricated, looking shifty.

"Don't mess with me, do you know where she is?" Barked Nicholas.

"Well, I did direct her to see the pictures some time ago." The guard said innocently.

"Show me?" Growled Nicholas.

"Well, that way." He pointed to the door she had gone through.

They rushed to the door that opened onto a small lobby without any apparent way through but Nicholas saw that the panel in front of him swiveled and he pushed it open hearing cries of distress. He saw Georgiou astride Carole slapping her around the face. His member was thrusting above her and Nicholas and Ian heard her moans of terror and pain.

With murder in his heart he rushed to her aid and realised his predicament. If he launched himself onto his tormentor they would be torn apart and in haste, to stop his enemy, might hurt her grievously.

He turned to Ian with a face of defeat and Georgiou looked up. With utter triumph, he looked at Nicholas. He rose slowly from his tumescent haven. His engorged member glistened with semen and he thrust it forward towards where Nicholas looked on in despair. He shrugged, his shrinking penis wet and shining. He laughed. "She's all yours, if you can satisfy her more than that!" And in one bound charged towards the two men. He floored Nicholas with his charge and turned towards Ian in casual contempt, thinking to have little difficulty dealing with him, but found that he had, unexpectedly, found a worthy adversary. They fought and lunged with bare knuckles in fair balance until Georgiou saw an opening and struck, only to find Ian neatly side step, and land a killer punch.

He went down in a crumpled heap. Ian looked closely at his opponent, making meticulous detailed examination of his inert figure, giving Nicholas time to see to Carole and gather her up.

Lifelessly she lay in his arms whilst he rocked her lovingly. "Caro, Caro, my darling what have I done to you? Oh Caro, Caro." He whispered his pleas into her hair with his face, truly ugly in its anguish.

Meanwhile Ian kept his gaze averted and had taken off Georgiou's tie and secured his hands together, then pulling the coat halfway off his shoulders to restrict his movements. He then unbuttoned the man's belt and tied his feet together looping his legs up behind his back and through his hands, tied with a half hitch over the end of the leather holes. He ran to fetch a blanket and call for assistance from Steve and Alan, leaving Nicholas to his private agony.

Nicholas gathered her lifeless form into the warm blanket and prayed that her life would be spared. There was very little vitality left in her and her bruises were plain to see. There would be others that only doctors must see. Shame, his agony, that he had failed to protect her. He had known the stakes were high but he had expected Georgiou to attack him. Well he had certainly done that, and had achieved his moment of triumph. And Nicholas' heart was breaking at the pity of it.

****

Ian helped Nicholas to take Carole into the front garden, to a bench under the shade of a cedar tree, and then took Steve and Alan Southgate to arrest Georgiou for the rape, and prayed it would not be for murder, as well.

The fireworks were at their height and shone over the water. Everyone was intent on their brilliance when, between them, they took Carole to the limousine that Ian and she had arrived in. They gently placed her in the back seat of the limousine in Nicholas's arms and Ian drove, to a private clinic, two miles away, as swiftly as he was able. Nicholas placed her in the care of two nurses and sat down with his head in his hands and awaited some news.

She appeared to be in a catatonic state where nothing could reach her. Although she had recovered consciousness she appeared to be sleepwalking. Nothing he said, seemed to get through to her and he feared for her sanity. He sat there with head bowed and thought about how this had happened and what they might face. He acknowledged that in his own disordered state, he had relaxed his vigilance on the scene, and had supposed that Carole was not a spectator to the action. He reflected, that perhaps Ian might also have been riveted to the scene, and possibly not aware of her 'retreat.' If she had left the garden because of what she had seen, the truth of his play-acting, then her distress might have led to the awful scene he had witnessed.

He knew that Georgiou was taking vengeance and would have found any opportunity to wound him.

He faced his faults fair and square and accepted his part in her brutal attack. He couldn't have anticipated Carole's reaction. When she realised the authenticity of his 'acting', she had just wanted to get away from the scene in front of her. But the reality was, that he had failed her.

He knew that he had found his father in an abject state of health and he had nursed him back to health.

He had returned to her, battered in body and changed of face and she had restored his dignity and given him unreserved love. Now he vowed that he would have the strength and love to restore her crushed and shamed body and restore her mind to its full state of health and he lifted up his soul to God, in a way he had not done since he was a child, and his father had been taken from him, and stumbling, he began.

Our Father who art in Heaven

Forgive my trespasses as I

Forgive those who trespass against me

And lead me not into temptation

But deliver me from evil. Amen. [sic]

"If my will be done, oh Lord, I will repay," he whispered in his desolation.

PART TWO

CONSEQUENCES

CHAPTER 1

Return from Geneva

Janice Murray had spent the most marvelous six months of her life during her time in Geneva. It was hard for her to think that it would shortly be coming to an end. She knew that by July, she would be returning to London for the rest of the year.

Every day had been different. There were many advantages to the position Geneva held in European affairs. Everyone seemed to pass through the city, and she had done her share of entertaining and being entertained, and had dealt with many important people. with tact and efficiency.

She had certainly become more poised and polished than in her London days. She had grown her hair so that she was able to vary the styling and had learnt to tease her hair much straighter to give it a slick finish but inevitably the rain made it spring into unruly curls again.

She thought of her friend, Carole, with whom she had shared a flat, and wondered whether she was still living in Chelsea. She had enjoyed their time together as flat-mates even though they had become involved in the 'mystery of the pearls'. Carole had been more closely involved, as she

164

had fallen hopelessly in love and when visiting Janice in Geneva, had been very unhappy.

Janice still felt that her decision to keep the lovers apart had been the right one, as Nicholas was just embarking upon an almost impossible challenge and didn't need the complication of his tangled love life.

She had been amazed and relieved at the success of her plan as they had all been staying at the same hotel.

She wondered whether Carole would still want her as a friend when she discovered her involvement in those few days in Geneva.

I suppose, she thought, it rather depended on her present relationship and whether things had ended happily for Carole. She had heard that the project that had taken Nicholas to Russia, had been successful. That he was back in England, and had been hurt but was recovering.

She sighed when thinking about her part in events. and acknowledged that she would have to 'face the music' on these relationships, as they might all be working together in the near future.

****

Sir Charles Willingham Wright, Head of European Ops at MI5, was recovering from a rather large lunch at his London Club, deep in a capacious armchair after more than usual amounts of alcohol. It was always thus, when he was dining with Buzz Berkeley, his American opposite number. His guest's insistence upon bourbon and cigarettes with everything, was rather too rich for Sir Charles. That left him imbibing more than was good for him in the wine stakes, and he knew that he would suffer from dyspepsia later.

However, it was very pleasant to enjoy the alcoholic haze for a little while longer, to contemplate the information that Buzz had imparted.

He had been amazed and astounded at the success of the investment they had made in recovering this propaganda tool, writer, Stefan Baronski. He had always thought that his son, Nicholas Baron had great potential and, here he was, having delivered the goods, battered and frail in body and mind, but Sir Charles felt no remorse for his part in things.

He was a servant of the State and, as such, he was not allowed the luxury of personal sentiment.

His task had always been to sift and analyse and send others to do the probing and searching. He must come up with likely links in a chain of circumstances and use his intuition in making sense of these random pieces of information. He had found this last asset, intuition, a hard tool to manage, as it was not in his nature to jump to conclusions, but that was often the only way connections were made. His strength lay in his ability to be a good judge of men and to use their personal characteristics to the best advantage.

He lit another cigar, and here he paused to congratulate himself, as he had been more than happy about his assessment of Nicholas Baron. He had seen him as a single-minded leader of men and he had heard plenty about that, from Buzz, and been very pleased with the first-hand information he had been able to obtain from both Stefan and Nicholas. He was happy that for once the 'Yanks' could be beholden to the 'Brits' for something as they were always rubbing it in that they had saved us from Hitler in WW2.

This time, the information they had received, might just save them from President Kruschev and his overwhelming ambition.

The fact that the American had been very instrumental in securing both Nicholas and Stefan for the sea-crossing, had quietly slid to the back of his memory. In fact, he did think it was a 'damned good show,' and was mightily relieved. Sir Charles felt he could enjoy this last cigar.

CHAPTER 2

Old Acquaintances

Late June.

Alex Counter, step-brother to Nicholas Baron, arrived at Winchester train station from Southampton with three times the luggage he had set out with.

He had arrived at Southampton on the ocean liner, 'Queen Elizabeth' after spending six months in America.

He had been working on a Texas ranch owned by one of his father's customers. His father, Tasha, was a manufacturer of boat engines and his trade with American customers went back to the beginning of his business after WW2, with G.I.s, returning to their farms or rivers. They had then wanted up-to-date machinery to work their farms and inland waterways.

Alex had found many artifacts that related to work that he was eager to show his father.

Home from America, Alex returned with a different perspective on his home country and was struck with the same wonder that other travelers returning home, had felt.

He was returning to a green and pleasant land. The wide, open spaces of Texas, made their little fields and disordered rambling lanes, seem like a form of toy-town, Now, he viewed the returning summer and all its hidden delights with more appreciation than ever before.

His father, Tasha, drove them up to St. Catherine's Hill and headed for Davidstown. The late afternoon light cast magical shadows over the undulating hills and every bend in the road gave way to another rolling view. Southwards, the Downs fell away to the Solent and all the bustle of a busy shipping port. Further beyond still, the Isle of Wight could be seen on a clear day. Everywhere the evening light picked up the colours and found depths of reflected light.

Father and son grinned at each other as Tasha, looked with wonder at the transformation. With his cowboy hat and denim jeans Alex looked every bit a cowboy. He had acquired a deep tan and muscles stretched tight inside his shirt after a summer working the animals. Testing his strength on all the tasks that were required on the ranch.

As they arrived at their farm on the downs, he heard a lark high in the sky, shrilling a welcome home, and the swifts circling and swooping trying to join the lark but not quite reaching his glorious ascent. Alex, eyes closed, took a deep breath and the sweet earthy verdure of the slopes assailed his nostrils.

"It's good to be home." He said to his father and they

169

smiled at each other, in perfect accord.

Deep into the night they talked about his trip, until Tasha mentioned that they were to expect some different horses soon – from Russia, and his mother, Minka, left them for his father to tell him what had happened to Nicholas.

"Yes, would you believe it, by all things wonderful, Nicholas has brought some horses, natives to the Steppes, for us to breed from. He thinks they have some potential as Polo horses with their strong chests and nimble feet. What do you think of that?"

"The crafty son of a gun." Alex exclaimed with his new Texan drawl. "What a fantastic opportunity to try something new Dad. But how did he manage that and where are they? Can we go to see them tomorrow?"

"Hang on, hang on, first they are still in quarantine, so we must be patient before we have them here. Some of them have foals with them, so there are difficulties there to curb your enthusiasm. We shall have to think a little more long-term than you might expect. How they came here, is a long story, which I am sure Nicholai will recount to you. In the meantime, I must tell you that Nicholai has come back much changed by his experience. He has successfully rescued his father, but apart from that, we do not yet know anything of his time in Europe, other than he was injured and is recovering. He is much changed by his journey and you must not tire him, when you meet."

"Why, what has happened to change him so? What could change Nicholas? He always succeeds when he sets his mind to triumph!"

"Aye, so we always believed, and it is true this time." Tasha was silent for a moment. "He has sustained a cruel wound to his face and is much changed in appearance. In time, of course, it will improve, but right now he is hiding away from the world."

"Oh, poor Nico, will he not even want to see me?"

"Well, that might not be true, but he did not contact me for some time after he had returned. I understand that he has become very reclusive. I went to see my friend Stefan and he was concerned at Nicholai's reluctance to leave London!"

"Where is he living?"

"Well he has a small Victorian house across the river from Chelsea."

"What!" Alex exclaimed. "Well I suppose he could not have taken his father to the boat. But then, it is near enough to his old area to come across the river if he chose to."

"Indeed, and he did ask if he might use the flat for a short while, for a friend, whilst his boat went to be refitted."

"What? Has his boat been occupied since he went away?" He queried.

"Apparently, although I don't know who is using it."

"Why should he feel obligated to his tenant to provide accommodation at this moment? I should have thought he had enough to think about without bothering to rehouse a tenant in rather better accommodation than his boat...unless...Do you know who it is?" Alex asked with a suspicion of whom it might be.

"Well actually, it was handled by the Letting agents but, now you come to mention, this was rather a strange request, because it was Nicholas who asked me. He seemed rather anxious that I should say yes."

"I knew it, I knew it. Said Alex laughing, "The sly fox. I bet I know who has taken up residence in the boat. Oh, I do hope so!" and he jumped up and danced excitedly round the room.

"Sit down. What are you saying?" Said Tasha, mystified.

'Well." Said Alex, taking his seat in the old leather armchair and bending towards his father confidentially. "You remember the young lady who was at the heart of the pearls affair, at the very beginning of this episode?"

"Yes." His father said slowly.

"Well, in all the years that Nicholas has been breaking hearts, I have never seen him 'smitten' as he was by her – indeed, I guess it was mutual, as the night he left, they definitely went out of the 'The Eagle and Flagstaff' together."

"Good Lord, God help him then." Tasha exclaimed soberly. "You might just be right, as there was definitely some reason why he was staying put, across the river. There had seemed no reason for remaining in London. I couldn't think why he would not come to us here."

"I suppose, Alex said, that he might be reluctant to meet her again, if he is as defigured as you say."

"That might certainly be a reason, for his wound is presently looking very livid and has quite changed his looks." His father said thoughtfully. "I think we should call it a day now, but perhaps we can think of some way to help him, in the morning."

With the bourbon, much depleted, it went back into the cupboard and Alex was left to wonder at the news. He resolved to see Nicholas for himself.

CHAPTER 3

Reflections

Nicholas was thankful that Otto had managed to get his father and himself away from Leningrad and onto the 'Ice Maiden'. He was surprised at how useful Otto was around horses, as they would have found looking after them, almost impossible without him.

He had even taken over the disembarkation and their removal to quarantine quarters and he felt more than ever that here was a real friend.

He had needed to completely re-evaluate his relationships, because of his uncle Dimitri's revelation. Nicholas had always believed he was his father's only son, and had been happy to renounce his theoretical inheritance of the farm near Samara, to his 'cousin,' because he had been farming it so long. Now Nicholas knew himself to be the younger son, and that the antagonism he had felt towards his 'cousin' had been one of sibling rivalry. Mikhail was now acknowledged as the older son, his half-brother, not his cousin.

His father's later renunciation of his bastard son was so appalling, yet Nicholas could not feel any pity for him.

His 'cousin's' anger had resulted in his own injury and, more importantly, the possible destruction of Mikhail's legal father Dimitri, in the stabbing, that had occurred on the quayside.

Otto had told him that his uncle had not died there, but he had no more news than that an ambulance had been called. Nicholas felt all the certainties of his life had crumbled. Before the relationship to his father and now a half-brother, were revealed, he had a rightful place beside his father. Now, all that, had been blown away by the revelations of that moment, before the knifing.

He felt he was floating on a cloud of uncertainties and the only thing that was real to him, was his love for Carole. Yet he felt he could not reach her, with his other reality of disfigurement. All he knew now, was that he couldn't let go of that physical contact, and had spent many hours watching her morning activities from across the river.

He had since taken his invisible presence to a new level by leaving obscure messages. This made his situation more absurd by the day, yet he held back revealing himself for fear of her reaction to his changed appearance.

Stefan had tried to distance him from the situation by trying to get him into the country and he had taken a cottage in the village of Avonbridge, Carole's hometown This had resulted in greater frustration when he had seen Carole enjoying her weekend with old friends. He had seen that she was trying to make another life, and he would lose her anyway, if he stayed away much longer.

CHAPTER 4

Crossed Paths

Alex woke the morning after his return home to England and went for a ride over the downs. The sun was behind banks of cloud and the wind was very light, with little hope of later sunshine. He saddled his gelding and adjusted to an American style of riding although his stirrups were not quite long enough to stretch completely but he wanted to try out this different position.

Up behind their barns, the downs stretched eastwards and he smelt the early morning air, so different to that which he had experienced in Texas. The grass was now as dry as it ever is and still the smell of moist grass persisted. The Downland flowers of heather, harebells and scabious tossed their heads as he galloped over them.

Two hours in the saddle and he had reached Melbon Valley. He reined in his mount. He walked the horse slowly across a plateau and galloped him down a gentle slope to the villages tucked into its steep sides. At Meon, he stopped to water his horse and eased his horse's girth at the village trough. He was in no hurry on this fine summer morning and went into the Post Office. He bought some airmail letters, a pack of biros and a bag of toffees, and was hailed by a female voice. "Well, what a nice surprise. It's Alex, isn't it? Where have you been hiding?" And he recognized the voice of Sheila Sterling, one of the party that had been at the Arts Ball. Of course, her parents lived in the village and he could not avoid her greeting but he cursed under his breath. He had not liked her attitude to their friend Boris who had died at the Chelsea Arts Ball, when she had thought that he was drunk, and considered her very petty.

"Oh, hello Sheila. Are you here to visit your parents?"

"Well actually yes and no, I'm just off to a cricket match. Do you care to join us later, 2 p.m. at UDCC, there'll be some of the crowd from London down for the weekend. Do come."

"I'll see. I have only just got back from Texas and am giving my horse a bit of exercise, but thanks anyway."

"What about your brother, is he down too?"

"Well actually I've only just arrived so haven't seen him since Christmas. We all have different lives now, don't we?"

"Mm…I don't. It's still the same old crowd. Anyway, good to see you and remember 2 00 p.m. We'll probably end up at the George and Flagstaff this evening."

He sidled out of the door without commitment and

was relieved to get away. That girl was so pushy, but maybe he might look in on the match later.

He arrived back home as the clock on the stable copula struck twelve, having meandered by fields of standing corn and through woods and meadows, savouring all the varied aspects of his local pastureland. He was in no hurry to take up his old life.

The meeting with Sheila had reminded him of his brother, and in what way, he might be able to help him. He remembered what Nicholas had whispered when he had last seen him. 'Trust Janice.' What had he meant by that? Was Nicholas involved in something more than the Chevaliers de Russie's original intention? The more he examined the different aspects of the case, the more it was clear to him, that Nicholas was into something much deeper than he had imagined. He half guessed his father was involved in more than he knew, and now Nicholas seemed to be ensnared also.

As he slowly made his way home, it seemed to him, that his only way forward was through Janice. Hadn't Nicholas said. "Trust Janice." So, he must try to contact her. They had exchanged brief postcards, she from Geneva, and he from Texas. More on his part anyway, as an antidote to his frustrations over all the nubile Texan girls who remained out of reach.

He knew that she was in the Foreign Office and would be back, about the same time as himself, for they had both left England at approximately the same time. But where could he contact her now?

By the time he returned home, Alex had resolved what must be done, and was more than able to do justice to his mother's cooking, for his appetite had increased enormously whilst running the herds in Texas.

CHAPTER 5

Return to England

Janice had just one more day in Geneva, then had to clear her desk. All her cases were packed and she was to fly to London, then Edinburgh for two weeks holiday with her parents.

Waiting on her desk was a letter unopened, and she recognised Alex's handwriting. It was not often she saw a handwritten letter these days and wondered why he should be writing more than the postcards he usually sent. Her boss had already arrived and she put it in her pocket in some confusion. She was rather glad he had written to her more intimately than on just a postcard, but could not imagine what he might say to her.

He had been rather a shy young man with very little small talk. When he spoke of things he knew about, she had found him good company.

He also loved skiing and they had compared their favourite resorts. He had never been to Scotland and she staunchly defended the skiing there. Weekends on the slopes around Geneva had given a wider view of what variety there was, but her loyalty had still been with the Scottish resort at Aviemore.

After the flurry of goodbyes and embarking on her flight, Janice finally settled to read her letter.

Dear Janice,

I hope you do not mind my writing to you like this, but I am uncertain how to proceed in my wish to contact Nicholas.

I believe that you might know more about his involvement in the 'Boris Affair', than might have been apparent at Christmas and could perhaps, enlighten me about the current situation.

I wonder whether you have kept contact with your flat-mate Carole. I suspect that she may be the reason he has 'gone to ground'.

I am particularly anxious about him as, during his time away in Europe, he sustained a defacing injury, that has greatly altered his looks and I think that Carole may be the key to his full recovery.

I apologise if I am speaking out of turn here, and please ignore this, if you have no more news than me, but I was given a last- minute directive by Nicholas to 'trust

Janice' so perhaps my intrusion into your busy life, is not entirely unwarranted.

I hope you are enjoying your time in Geneva, which if I remember, must be nearly over, as indeed, is my trip to Texas. Fabulous!

Hope you are well and look forward to any piece of news you can give me.

Your friend,

Alex

She read it through twice to absorb the facts:

1) Nicholas had made it back to Britain.

2) He had been brutally injured.

3) He was hiding away.

4) Was Carole the cause of this?

5). Alex knew she might know more than could be expected.

Erm ... well that was true, but at this moment she knew only that he had embarked upon his journey and she had kept the two lovers apart.

She now knew that Nicholas had made it home...with

or without his father? But…was his reclusiveness anything to do with Carole?

She remembered the dinner they had shared in Geneva when he had asked her to be their friend. Well. at the time, she had thought that the best chance of success in his venture, had been to put any thought of Carole behind him. But what now? The circumstances of his return were very different. Would Carole be interested in a maimed man, but what exactly was that injury? Would she be helping Carole, to drag her back into a relationship, which might not be in her best interests? She pondered this information but had not decided her course of action when they began to descend to Heathrow Airport.

****

Two days later Minka and Tasha had received an invitation to the Bastille Day Celebrations at Richmond and there was a buzz of expectation about the house. Minka, of course, was excited in the way of all women. and was already enjoying the anticipation, and asked all sorts of questions about the event.

It was to be an afternoon party with evening fireworks, in either formal or fancy dress, and was to take place at a rather interesting historical house on the river at Orchard Hill, Richmond, built originally by an 18th century literary figure and Prime Minister's son.

"Will you come with us Alex, I am sure there will be

many interesting people there?" "Em...I'm not sure, I may have to go elsewhere that weekend, I'll let you know." He said vaguely.

He had hoped that any day soon he would receive a letter from Janice. and was surprised to find that he was eagerly looking forward to renewing their acquaintance. He had thought her a rather serious young woman, with none of the more obvious charms of her friend, but she was intelligent and thoughtful, and had proved a sensible friend for Carole.

She had a full Scottish accent, that was evenly modulated, and her freckles and curly auburn red hair had nearly echoed his own unruly auburn curls.

He had been given until the end of July to sort out his college work, and his father had suggested that he came to the factory to see what the situation was there. They did a lot of work with Americans in the Everglades and Mississippi delta, and any inland waterways in the same region of the southern states. They produced light two-stroke engines that could be transferred from boat to land, and were very easy to use and maintain. These were sold to many countries that relied on water travel for distribution and communication.

He had an idea for a flat-bottomed boat, to be used with this engine, as many of the boats that used them were dug-outs or canoes, and a flatter bottomed boat would be more stable and perhaps be used with greater versatility. He had come back fired with ideas and was keen to experiment, but for the moment he wanted to seek Nicholas out.

They had always bounced ideas off each other and he was concerned that Nicholas was not his usual self, hiding away from people.

Another week went by, and Alex decided to seek out the Cricket Club crowd. He was reluctant to see Sheila again but thought he might get some news of Nicholas from them.

As he drew away from the house, a car turned into their drive. He saw an old man in the passenger seat and a bearded man at the wheel, then he was passed and idly wondered who they were. He was glad to be back in his old M.G. and the afternoon drive was just as he remembered it. Then it hit him. Of course, it must be Nicholas and his father…and he had not recognized him! Could that really have been the case? What had he seen of the man at the wheel? Well not much, he had to concede, but he had seemed an older man with grey streaked hair and…He thought, but he could only remember the beard. He slowed the car to a stop and meant to turn around. Then he thought better of it. Perhaps it was best to meet them one by one as, if it was his father with him, there would be an emotional moment, without Alex adding to it. He conceded. No perhaps it was better to see him later, and they could go out for a couple of hours to the pub and catch up there. He was far more likely to hear what had happened if there were just the two of them, he thought. So, he revved up the M.G. and proceeded to the cricket match.

Later he returned home from the day's play and looked for another car in the drive but there was none in sight. Damn. He thought. Have they gone already? He had automatically assumed that Nicholas would be staying. In his haste, he jumped out of the open topped car, without opening the door, and went swiftly into the house.

"Anyone around." He called and his mother drew him into the lounge.

"Alex, come along and meet our visitor. May I introduce my son Alex to you Stefan, and Alex, this is Nicholas's father who you will know has come far to meet us." She said in an excited voice.

He came forward and recognised the old gentleman fleetingly seen in the car, who was now sitting in front of a FIRE in the middle of July and he bent to shake his hand! He saw how frail the man was.

"Welcome to our home, Papa Stefan, if I may call you that, for that is how you have always been known to me?"

"Of course, of course, I am happy to know you. You are just as Nicholas has described, except a little bit older than I imagined, for you are not a boy but a man!"

Alex laughed. "Well Nicholas always regards me as his little brother." He paused. "Where is Nicholas, by the way?"

His mother was frowning. "I am afraid he has already

gone. He asked that we look after Stefan for a while and indeed he is a most welcome guest." She came forward and put her arm around the man's shoulders. "Nicholas could not stay as he had some urgent business in London, but has promised to telephone us soon." She said in a troubled voice. He could see that she had a worried look on her face but he forebore to press her.

"Well, I am very cross with myself because I had passed the car as I left the house, and only when I was on my way, did I realise that it must be Nicholas and you Sir. I thought that he would automatically be here as well, and as I was on my way for a particular time, I had thought to catch up with him later."

Stefan looked at him straight from blue eyes, Nicholas' eyes. "Yes, it is understandable that you did not immediately recognise your brother, as he is much altered." And he held Alex's gaze steadily.

So, I have a lot to prepare myself for, he thought.

"We are all so sorry to hear of his injuries, but I must congratulate him on the success of his mission in bringing you here to Britain. That was a great achievement. You have a fine son, Papa Stefan, and I have been lucky to call him brother for the past ten years."

"You gladden my heart to hear that, as I have been

much saddened by revelations…that we learnt in Samara and it is good that he can count…on one brother…at least."

Alex opened his mouth to query Stefan's words but something held him back. No, whatever had happened, it was for Nicholas to tell him, he thought.

Minka, his mother, with a catch in her voice said. "Yes, let's put these things past, to one side for a moment."

"Stefan, perhaps you would like a small walk with Alex around the garden, as there is a lovely view to be had over the downs, and he will, perhaps, show you his beloved horses."

"That would be very good, but I fear it will have to be more looking than walking, as I have very little strength yet." And taking the proffered arm, they went to see the sunset over the downs.

****

Later, Stefan had gone to his room to unpack and await Tasha before dinner. Alex found his mother in the kitchen preparing the meal. He could see that she was upset and put his arms around her shoulders.

"What's up, Ma." He asked, as he could see that she had been crying.

"Oh, Alex, what a mess, I have seen Nicholas for the

first time since his return and it is an awful shock. He has a livid scar from eyebrow to chin and he has obviously been in a lot of pain. He had lost so much weight and oh, Alex, he's no longer my smiling, charming boy, but hardened of face, and seemingly tortured of soul. I cannot make out what is troubling him as he has done what he set out to do and his injury will heal somewhat, in time, but it seems he wants to keep us at a distance, which is so unlike him. I know that Tasha wants to help and is more than happy to have Stefan here, but why won't Nicholas come home?"

"Perhaps this has more to do with who else he is hiding from."

"What do you mean?" Minka asked.

"Well, I might be on completely the wrong tack, but I think Nicholas fell in love at Christmas."

"But that's wonderful." Interrupted Minka.

"Perhaps, but there were a lot of complications. I don't need to remind you of his purpose, and I think he fell in love with the young lady involved in the exchange of pearls, and perhaps will she have forgiven him for the deception? After all, there were some decidedly dodgy aspects to the plan. There was the sudden death of Boris to be reckoned with, and she was pitched right into a scheme which did not show Nicholas in a very good light. The fact that he probably fell in love for the first time was complicated by his instructions to use her as a decoy."

"Will he want to face her in the present circumstances? Oh, it really is a mess, isn't it?"

CHAPTER 6

Something must be done

Meanwhile, Carole and Nicholas were embarking upon the two weeks idyll, forced upon them by their duties, which had successfully cemented their relationship. Then, oh then, oh so briefly, when they had been thrown together by their involvement in the Basildon House surveillance that had ended so tragically for Carole.

A miracle fortnight of reunion and renewed love. He had held back from declaring total commitment because of their need to concentrate on the job they had been assigned by Sir Charles. This had blown asunder all their hopes and dreams, and Nicholas had resolved to do everything in his power to help her recover from the appalling attack he had witnessed.

Week followed week and her mental state had steadied and an improvement was more marked, but his own anguish was held in check by a thread.

Unbeknown to Alex, Janice was being briefed by Sir Charles when taking up her post again in Whitehall, after the Bastille Day Celebrations.

It was clear to Sir Charles that the 'call girl' debacle would have dire consequences for the Government and he was in the process of a damage limitation exercise. He was glad that Janice had returned just when he needed her, as his operative at the Bastille celebrations had been submitted to a gross attack by Georgiou Kadinsky. He cursed at his inability to progress this crime. Powerful members of the Russian Embassy had claimed immunity for the miscreant. Deportation was the most Sir Charles could hope for. It was particularly galling when there were two reliable witnesses to the attack who would have given impeccable evidence. But which would also have opened up a scene to both Ian and Nicholas to confirm. Painful in the extreme.

When his rational mind took over, he reflected that at least it spared Carole from any court proceedings. However, it was not a satisfactory conclusion for justice would not be served.

Carole had been staying at a nursing home/psychiatric clinic since the attack and there was no question of her returning to work for some time.

Thus, Janice had come back at just the right moment and she was soon 'au fait' with events. She read the brief with growing concern for both Nicholas and Carole.

Alex had obviously been right in suspecting Nicholas's motive for going to ground, but had been thrown together with Carole, in the most unexpected way.

He now seemed to be fully absorbed in caring for Carole and Janice's heart was touched by his devotion to the girl.

It seemed that absence really had made the 'heart grow fonder' but they both, now, had problems to surmount and she did not envy them, for life had thrown a bucketful of troubles in their way.

She now felt ready to write to Alex but how much should be revealed?

Some of these events were not hers' to tell. She did think that Alex could be helpful rather than the reverse and she also felt that she must help Carole to regain full health.

With this in mind, she decided to invite Alex up to London to speak to him about events. She wasn't sure how long he would want to stay up in town, but remembered that his father had a London flat at Dolphin Square.

****

Alex received Janice's letter with a glad heart. He was surprised at how eagerly he had looked forward to her letter.

He still did not know where Nicholas was, and Stefan was still staying with them. He had begun to take more interest in life and in his talks with Alex, they had ranged over many aspects of political life. He saw how like Nicholas he was in many ways, but there was a political conviction bordering on mania in his talks. Alex accepted that this was understandable, if not wise, after his incarceration in the Gulag. He tried to bring Stefan up to date with some of the realities of the 1960s but it was difficult for him to comprehend this changed world. He had begun to talk of writing a book and Alex thought that might channel his convictions more clearly. He had also been persuaded to go to the Bastille Event but had come back rather querulous, as he had not seen Nicholas, who was supposed to be there on business.

Tasha and Minka had come back from the fireworks and were surprisingly subdued about the event. They also had not seen Nicholas, but had met Sir Charles Willingham-Wright, an old acquaintance of Tasha, who had some news at last of Nicholas. He was engaged on business matters and would be out of touch for some time. Sir Charles promised. "to pass on." their good wishes, but was non-committal about anything else, and they had to be content with that.

Now, at the beginning of August, Janice had written back and Alex tore the letter open.

Dear Alex,

Lovely to hear from you again with a little more content than the postcards exchanged! It was with consternation that I heard your news, as I had last seen Nicholas in Geneva, when he was about to embark on his journey. He had seemed well and ready for his quest, but definitely lovesick.

It was brought home to me, upon reading his file, that should he visit Geneva that week in January, any distractions might jeopardize his mission. Since Carole had come with me to have a week's holiday, I had a job keeping them apart.

She also seemed very sad at his departure, but I had tried to lift her spirits by days out, etc., and had managed to do so and could not see any useful purpose in arranging a meeting. He needed to concentrate; and she needed to get on with her life. If that sounds callous, I apologise, but I was thinking in my professional capacity.

On his last night we dined formally, and he asked if Carole was well and after some prevarication I managed to stay just to the right side of the truth and he asked me to 'be her friend' and then "I hope you will be my friend also." On reflection, I truly thought that I had been, and indeed, still am. But they may not view my actions in the same light. You must judge.

Now that I am back in England I have reason to know more about them, since Nicholas and his father have been back, and I am not sanguine about their future happiness.

If you would like to meet me in London, at your convenience, I would welcome your help and support in ensuring, the future happiness of two people, we both hold in high esteem.

I truly look forward to seeing you again as I really think 'two heads are better than one' in this regard.

Yours,

Janice

P.S. My telephone at home is...

Phew! That was some letter from Janice. He thought. It was masterly.

She had admitted nothing yet had told everything.

1) She definitely had Foreign Office connections with Nicholas.
2) She was his minder in Geneva.
3) She knew of his quest.
4) Nicholas was in love.
5) Carole was in love? Perhaps but best not to be.
6) They were reunited! but in what circumstances?
7) Outcome uncertain? Why, but he could see that Janice was sufficiently aware of present circumstances to fear for their happiness.

What had she said. 'not sanguine about their future happiness.' What did that mean? Together, or even apart?

He resolved that he would go to London in two days' time on the first Saturday in August.

CHAPTER 7

Meeting with Janice

The fields sped past and Alex could enjoy the changing landscape from above the roads, as the train gave way to the urban sprawl. He reflected that, the same distance in Texas, had been without interruption to the view for mile upon mile, but here, there was a microcosm of humanity from town to country, town to country, town to country, as he rattled over the points. But soon he was at Clapham Junction and he left the train and his reflections.

He had decided to ask for the use of the flat. He had initially, been rather reluctant to mention his visit, but he spoke privately to his father about his intentions and was extremely glad he had done so, for he could hear the relief in his father's voice. "Just bring him home." Tasha whispered.

"I don't know if I can do that Pa, but I am seeking news of him," and they had left it at that.

He took a cab to Chelsea Harbour, and left his overnight bag at the flat, putting his night-clothes on the bed. He glanced around the room and saw a packet next to the side of the bed with a Harrods label on it. Intrigued, he looked inside, and stopped, realising that it was a woman's very sexy nightdress, and couldn't imagine his mother wearing it.

What on earth? He felt he had stepped into a very private moment and didn't know how to proceed. He looked in the wardrobe and saw that someone had left some clothes. Definitely not his mother's…He remembered what his father had said about Nicholas wanting to use the flat for a tenant? He remembered his suspicions then, and now, here was evidence of occupation. Had he stepped into someone else's flat? He looked at the wardrobe and could imagine Carole in some of these clothes.

He went into the lounge and everything was neat and tidy, but in the kitchen, there was a dirty coffee cup in the sink which held some coffee dregs covered in mold and in the fridge, there was food that had obviously been there far too long.

What had happened? The tenant had obviously left as though for the day but had not returned. Where was she…? He knew that it was a woman, but…was it Carole?

He went into the master bedroom but everything that he recognised, was in order. There were his mother's brushes and a pair of his father's shoes. In the wardrobe was a city suit and 'Crombie' coat. So, he was certain that those were his father's belongings.

He cleared the sink and emptied the food into the bin

and took it out to the chute. He looked again at the dressing table in his room and saw a bottle of perfume. He smelt the distinctive smell of Chanel No.5 and remembered the time when they had lain Carole on the bunk bed and he recognised the scent. It was the same and he felt his suspicions confirmed.

He went down to the front desk and asked.

"I have just been up to No.15 and expected to see my cousin there but she seems to have left in a hurry. Do you have any forwarding address?"

"No.15, did you say, ah Miss Semele. Well no, as a matter of fact it's rather strange, I had a bunch of flowers delivered to her door but she never came back to collect them. When I looked for the message I couldn't find one. Bit strange that Sir, don't you think?"

"Well yes, very strange, I shall have to ask around at her place of work."

He left the flat and walked down to the river. He looked at the boats in the harbour but could not see any sign of Nicholas' boat. What the! He paused, this had some of the hallmarks of a secret tryst but could it have more sinister overtones?'

He was deeply troubled when he met up with Janice at the 'Chelsea Potter'.

He entered the bright pub and looked around for her

curly mop. He thought he was early until he glanced again, at a smartly dressed young woman at the corner table, who waved cheerily at him.

Janice? Is that Janice? As he bent to kiss her on the cheek he was conscious of a sudden pounding of his heart, as he was thrown into confusion by her sophisticated looks. Such poise and elegance, was not what he had remembered, and he needed all his new sense of assurance to come to his aid.

"What a lovely vision you are young lady," he rallied. "and where is the wee Scottish lassie I knew?"

She drew herself up and looked at him in mock distain.

"That was then. Now, I am a much travelled European." She said proudly.

"Ah. Oh dear, that was not the thing to say, was it? But you look all the lovelier for it anyway." He said, with more than a touch of the charm, that he had learnt from Nicholas.

"Well, I might say the same of you Alex. Where is the uncertain, gawky young man of yesteryear? Gone with a bevy of young Texan beauties, I'll be bound." She asserted.

"I wish." He said laughing. "There were plenty of those." He admitted. But they all hunted in twos, so I never got to sample any of them." He said honestly, and somehow, she was glad.

They settled down and ordered drinks and pie and chips and remembered their former life, chatting naturally, whilst they ate. Afterwards, Alex broached the subject of his anxiety.

"I am extremely worried about what has happened to Nicholas. He seems to have completely disappeared and we don't know how to contact him. If he wishes to remain so, there is nothing we could do about it, but perhaps you could enlighten me further if you are able to."

She lit a cigarette and puffed on it slowly. "Well, I'm not sure I can help you very much more. I can let you know that he is physically well, but emotionally he is not."

"Is it that damned girl?" He asked hotly, thinking that she had rejected the altered Nicholas.

'Shh, shh, don't get angry. No, you mustn't think ill, of her."

She paused, then continued. "Nicholas and Carole had been together for a couple of weeks and it might have resolved everything between them except, that, something came between them that they couldn't predict, and, she, she is, unwell." She ended feebly.

He looked at her puzzled. "What do you mean 'unwell'? Not because of Nicholas I hope?" And she realised that he was partly right, but could never tell him the whole story.

"Well, yes and no. I can't tell you more except that I hope for Nicholas' sake, she returns to good health."

"My God." He went pale. It can't be that Nicholas has hurt her?"

"No, no, he is not to blame but he feels responsible for…what has happened."

He shook his head again. "I don't understand, you are not making sense. In what way is Nicholas involved?"

She looked at him again and paused for a long time. "You could say that it was because she was loved by Nicholas that she is unwell but he had no part in causing her…pain." Still he did not understand but he felt relieved as it seemed his worst fears were unfounded.

"Well, it is still a mystery to me but it seems that you think we might do something to help?" He queried hopefully.

"Yes, I can only think that perhaps we should await events and not pressure Nicholas to explain things. He is struggling to help Carole at the moment and I don't think he wants any more fuss, but perhaps you might write an informal letter to him about your return and all the things of home. Reassure him that his father, Stefan, is well and that everything out there is NORMAL. They are enclosed in a world of their own at the moment, but a touch of reality could help him, I think."

"You have certainly set me thinking Janice, and I need another drink. What would you like?"

"A tonic will be fine for me." She said firmly and they went on to talk of other things.

He told her of the cricket match and of old acquaintances and the afternoon wore on.

They walked along the river to the harbour and he explained about the flat, hoping for more enlightenment, but there was nothing forthcoming

He was reluctant to leave her and suggested they went to see West Side Story. She had relocated to Belgravia and they stopped by her flat for her to change. He could see, that her prospects had improved since they had met previously, and he was impressed by her.

They walked towards Buckingham Palace and through the Mall, taking their time. It was a warm sunny evening and there were lots of people in the park. They sat on a park bench halfway to Trafalgar Square, and watched the pigeons.

Alex was aware that he wanted to put Nicholas and all his problems away from their conversation as he was acutely aware of the girl at his side. But how could he move on from here. He jumped up and pulled her to her feet.

"Come on, we have to be at the cinema in half an hour." And he held on to her hand which she didn't withdraw.

Two and a half hours later he had a weepy woman on his hands but he did not feel embarrassed and was sufficiently moved by the film himself, to hug her feelingly.

"Oh, such a lovely film." She blubbered.

"Yes, it certainly was." He agreed and tucked her hand under his arm and squeezed it. "I know a little Italian restaurant around the corner from here. Are you hungry?"

She nodded and was content to be led to this stand-by of 'exotic cuisine'. How many young couples of their generation had dated in such a way?

They ate their spaghetti and sat talking until they became aware that they were the last people in the restaurant.

He hailed a taxi, suddenly inadequate to the feeling surging through him. What had happened to him? Here he was with a lovely young woman he had thought of as a friend, and now he was feeling much more than just friendly towards her.

They climbed in and he took her hand in his again. "Such a small hand." He thought, although she matched him almost for height, but his sense of manliness brought out a protective streak towards this most practical of young women.

They arrived back at her flat and he walked her to her door. He hesitated on the doorstep but bent down to kiss her, lightly he had thought, but somehow it became more passionate and he was rooted to the spot. He stroked her hair and kissed her ear, and neck, and…he was in the grip of passion. He had never realised how this would affect him and he wanted it to go on forever.

With a start, he knew that this must stop, but he had felt no reluctance on her part. They withdrew and there was a dewy smile on her face as she looked at him.

"Janice, I'm sorry, I shouldn't have." And longing was in his face. She smiled at him and kissed him back, first shyly then repeated it until he was again her slave.

She accepted that here was a man she could truly give herself to. He had all the qualities she admired. and was not some artificial sophisticate that she had been resisting all Spring. Her time in Geneva had given her plenty of opportunities to sample love but she had resisted most overtures, except of a more casual kind, but suddenly she did not wish to resist. Here was a man she now wanted, to lead on to greater intimacy.

She held him slightly at bay and retrieved her key. She did not dare to let go of him, as she felt his uncertainty, but with door open, he followed her call and there was no more resistance in his actions.

He held her close and his hands slid down to her buttocks and pulled her close. She felt her abdomen lurch and she thrust herself closer to his body. She felt his arousal and delighted in her power.

Each was a novice, and every step was an experiment for them both. He unbuttoned her blouse and she did the same to him. As they peeled each layer, they explored each other's body. They were both holding back some control of the situation but at each new exploration, their hunger grew.

Alex was beyond thinking by now but some vestige of control was still his, and he wondered how long it would last. There had been no rejection of his advances and he resolved, he would go only where he was led.

Could she really trust him? he thought, and something inside him said yes. Here was a woman he could love if she would have him, and did not feel that this was an act of casual satisfaction. They lay side by side on a rug in front of the fire and gazed at each other. He traced the line of her jaw with his hand and looked at her alabaster body in front of him. Her nipples were as red as cherries and he touched them.

She lay facing him with the same entranced look on her face and saw his tanned and muscle hardened body in front of her, with his penis ready and she knew that this was the moment and there was no retreat.

She felt all her wetness ready for him but she was innocent of the act and did not know what to expect. She slowly turned on her back and pulled him gently to her. He rolled onto her and felt for an opening as she relaxed her legs to his bidding. She was aware of a piercing pain followed by a thrusting and she responded with arching back and quickening hunger and then the moment was passed and she held him helplessly still, in her arms.

She did not need to move. She was content to know that she had fulfilled his desire and she held the moment. With dazed eyes, and a look that she had not seen before, he began to focus on her face and withdrew.

"Janice, what have I done? Are you alright, I never knew?"

"Nor I." She said breathlessly, and he gathered her once more into his arms more eloquently than any words and she felt secure. They lay there until the sounds of London awoke them to their nakedness and she pulled him into her bedroom in her embarrassment. All thought of Nicholas and

Carole were far from their thoughts and they resumed their exploration of each other.

CHAPTER 8

Renewed Friendship

Sir Charles was finding his job very difficult. He had hoped that having Janice back in the office would solve his problems, as she was usually a very steady young woman, able to deal sensibly with his requests. But this morning she had arrived late and didn't seem fit for anything. Was she sickening? He hoped not, but she had seemed only half awake and he had to repeat requests several times.

By coffee time she had begun to focus and was able to respond to his questions about whether she had read the brief on Nicholas and Carole.

"Yes," she said. "What an awful story."

"Well, it certainly wasn't something we could have anticipated. She seemed such a sensible girl but it seems to have affected her badly. You were her flat-mate for a while, weren't you? I was wondering whether I could send you down to see her. This is obviously a very delicate situation but she must guess that her case will have been examined by someone here, especially as Ian dealt with it at the time." He stopped and hesitated.

"I feel reluctant to bring him in on this, for it is a bit of female company that might be more use to her now. I don't believe she has contacted her parents yet, so perhaps you might go and visit her instead?"

"As a matter of fact," said Janice. "I had thought the same but wasn't sure, if I was butting in where I shouldn't."

"Well, obviously this is not something she would want bandied about, but a female friend would help most, I think."

"What about her partner, Nicholas?"

"He has been distraught but is visiting her every day. This may or may not be the best situation as he is also in a highly emotional state. You will see that he also has been injured recently, twice as a matter of fact, as he had an infected dog bite two weeks ago."

"I am worried personally of course, but my main concern is from an operational viewpoint as there have to be questions in 'The House' before long. We cannot contain this news of a leak, much longer."

"I will go tomorrow afternoon if that is what you want." Offered Janice.

"Splendid. Now, can I have your attention for the rest of the day!"

****

Alex went back to Hampshire feeling as though he was nine feet into the clouds.

He did not become aware of his surroundings until they had passed Basingstoke and he began to count off the stations.

He arrived home, just as his father came back from the factory in Southampton, and Tasha raised his eyebrows in query. He gave his father a smile of reassurance, although he was far from feeling it.

Papa Stefan had been walking around the downs on his own and was looking very much better. His voice had a firmer ring to it but he was still expressing petulance at Nicholas's neglect.

"I have some news on that front Papa Stefan. I understand that Nicholas is unable to contact anyone as he is dealing with some very sticky problems for the Government, but sends his love to everyone."

Tasha looked at him sharply and Alex realised that he was not fooling him.

Later they shared a whisky and his father tackled him again.

"Now Alex, that explanation you gave Stefan and your mother won't wash. Can you tell me anything more?"

"Actually, I am left with a more disturbed sense of affairs than before."

"I wrote to Carole's friend Janice to see if she knew anything from a female angle, as they were flat-mates. Perhaps you remember her Sir, I think you met her at some political dinner?

I had kept in touch with her by postcard while I was in Texas, as she was posted to Geneva about the same time. Perhaps you remember a bonnie Scots lass." He said warmly and was acutely aware of blushing and having a different tone to his voice.

His father waited for more from him and he was aware that he had drifted off the point, in his contemplation of his love. "It seems she also can't tell me much, but she did seem concerned about them both and will try to let me know, if she is able to. But his absence is definitely connected with Carole."

"It is certainly true that she openly expressed her regard for him at the Bastille Event but then, complete silence." His father agreed.

Alex continued. "I understand that she is unwell but know nothing of the cause. Janice has promised to keep me informed, if there is any news."

His father grunted. "Well, I guess we will have to possess ourselves with patience."

"Now, may I ask a different question?" Said his father, looking at him keenly. Alex looked back at him and blushed. He was acutely aware of what was coming next. "What of this young Scottish lady you have mentioned? She seems suddenly to loom large on your horizon. Are we about to have you disappear as well?" He said sardonically.

He wondered how much he should tell his father, but he could not deny his involvement. He didn't want to deny it, but his feelings were still very new to him and, for the moment, too precious to shout from the rooftops.

"No. I don't think that is going to happen, but we are now, an item." And he looked at his father man to man.

Of course, it was as plain as a bell cord over his whole being, and his father could read all the signs. He was glad his son had found such a pleasant and sensible young woman to fix his affections upon, just as he was glad that it had not been a sassy Texan!

****

Janice left the office with relief. It was all she could do to keep her concentration. All she wanted, was to relive the weekend moments with Alex. She had been a fool to be so unaware of her interest in him, way before he had come last weekend, and now they had moved much faster than she could have imagined.

They had both had opportunities to explore any sexual encounters before this moment but had held back. Somehow, they had both decided to commit to this relationship. She had no doubt that they had both made their choice with a consciousness of the depth of their feeling, and it had not been an evening of pure passion. She remembered the shy young man she had known nine months ago and knew he had become the man she had made him, as he had made her the woman she had become.

She knew that she had experienced a very special weekend and she couldn't believe that she had been so blind. Now she must help him to find a way to assist Nicholas and here was a clear opportunity.

Tomorrow she would go to see Carole and perhaps see Nicholas at the same time. She had rung the clinic and explored their willingness to allow Carole a visitor. She emphasized the official nature of her visit as a colleague, meaning to take too much emotion out of her request. She suspected that Nicholas was probably Carole's only visitor at the moment and she regarded that as counter- productive. It was much healthier for her, to engage with the world again and, from an entirely unprofessional viewpoint, she thought that a visit from a woman friend would be good for her. Her, no nonsense Scottish view, was that the sooner she put it behind her, the better.

Carole had an adoring man at her side but it was not going to keep him there, if she couldn't 'snap out of it.' Thus, thought the voice of reason in 1962, and a strong sense of enduring life's vicissitudes was inherent in her highland character.

She had checked when Nicholas usually visited Carole, and planned to visit her before he was due. She did not mean to preach at Carole but thought it possible, that a bit of straight talking, might help.

She now knew the power of her own emotions and 'sometimes it was up to us to tip the balance. She thought sagely, as her moment of awakening had been driven as much by her desire as that of Alex, but it had been a fragile moment of decision and might never have happened if she had shown signs of resisting his passion.

But here, something different had happened. Carole had witnessed the charade being played out between Nicholas and Charlotte Kiel and had seen that the woman held more power over Nicholas than she wished to watch, and it had sent her running into danger.

Georgiou was watching for any opportunity to hurt Nicholas, and he had taken revenge by his twisted, gross and perverted course of action, and his anger had defeated Carole in the fight that had ensued. The fact that Nicholas had come upon the rape scene, was Georgiou's triumph, but

Carole's utter shame, and it was in this context, that she must try to counsel her friend.

She took a train to Richmond and then walked towards the river. The workers were streaming out of the offices to catch the sun shining over the summer scene. Small river craft, rowing boats and racing skiffs were out in plenty, and several ferryboats from down river were moored along the bank. She paused to look at the merry scene and the picture of normality that it represented and she was convinced that this was what Carole needed. Not being cooped up, and regarding herself as a pariah, to be shut away.

She greeted her friend with a friendly hug. "Carole, I am so glad you agreed to see me. You look well, but I think you need a bit of Scottish air in your lungs, because you are very pale."

"Oh Janice. Carole said with a tragic smile. You are just what I need to hear with your Scottish good sense. I feel I am cocooned in cotton wool here, and might never find my way out. Everyone is so kind that I feel guilty to want...want...oh I don't know?" She sat down and helplessly fluttered her hands.

Janice looked at her for a long minute. "It seems to me," she said slowly, "that what might have been good for you temporarily, is now making your progress more difficult. I understand that Nicholas visits you every day?"

"Yes, he has been so good, so patient.

"But?" asked Janice.

"Yes, but I feel that my life is on hold and I dare not go forward as I fear…fear…" And she was unable to proceed.

It seemed to Janice that she had been in this place, too long, with nothing but her own sorrows, to keep her company. Nicholas, bless him, had proved his devotion, but that would not be enough as Janice now knew from her own newly awakened sense of love for Alex.

"Tell me," she asked lightly, "have you to be signed off or can you discharge yourself?"

"I don't really know as everything was handled by Ian after the celebrations." She managed.

"Perhaps I might make a suggestion?"

Carole nodded.

"If you were invited to have a week's holiday in Scotland, would you consider coming there with me? I have yet to go to see my family, since coming back from Geneva. I would like you to come along as a bit of company and support, as I shall be besieged by my younger siblings. They are all lovely, of course, but are a bit overwhelming 'on masse,' but they are all very uncomplicated, and we can walk the hills and picnic by the burns, if you feel you can take such ordinary fayre."

"I am sure the mountain air will be good for you, but you must know, what you would be letting yourself in for."

Carole looked at her friend doubtfully remembering the half-holiday they had spent in Geneva. It would take her away from Nicholas of course, and she couldn't bear that thought, but perhaps he could also be released from his daily visits. If only, if only he doesn't abandon me. She thought forlornly.

Janice divined some of the turmoil Carole was thinking and said.

"By all accounts, Nicholas is like you, unable to think straight. But, I believe his love will not waiver. I cannot say more now, but, have good reason to know of his devotion, and he will not disappear again, if you spend some time in good mountain air. After all, she said hesitantly, you went home, more light of heart, after visiting me in Geneva, didn't you?" I understand that Nicholas will be here soon so, won't press you, but take a look at things from his angle, and see the torture you are putting him through."

Janice kissed and hugged her and did not allow any tears to fall. "If you want to come, it will take just a day to arrange in the office, and let's face it, Sir Charles is pining to see his 'Miss Semele' back in the fold." She said lightly.

"I will ring tomorrow. So, till then, bye." And she left Carole with ten minutes to ponder her suggestion before Nicholas was due to arrive.

She walked back across the river and finally saw what she was looking for along the riverbank. A newly painted cruiser moored some little way from the rest. It bore the title Northern Empress on its bows and she marked the time. She would take the opportunity to get some provisions and meet Nicholas as he headed back over the bridge. She had made her way back to the other side of the bridge, just as Nicholas came towards her. He faltered, and seemed uncertain whether to proceed. She saw that she had only known him because she knew of his injuries and was expecting the encounter. Otherwise, she would probably have passed him by. She continued towards him and, whilst some way off, smiled and greeted him.

"Nicholas, how good to see you again." She stopped and he was unable to walk past her, although she could see that he wished to avoid her.

"I won't detain you Nicholas as I know you are on your way to see Carole." He looked at her keenly.

"You know, of course, why wouldn't you?" He said reluctantly.

"Yes, and I have just been to see her. I just wanted to have this chance to speak to you also."

"I have invited her to come to Scotland soon to help her adjust to ordinary life and I think it will be better for both of you if you feel able to trust her to me. I know she is precious to you Nicholas, and that you would do anything to help her. But right now, your very solicitude might be holding her back. She needs to return to the normal world and here she is constantly reminded that she can't cope."

Nicholas stared at her with a thunderstruck look on his face as though it had never occurred to him, to think in this way.

"Don't say anything now Nicholas, because you will be late. I will be here in Richmond for a couple of hours and would like to come aboard your boat when you return, and bring you up to date on one or two things."

Nicholas nodded gravely unable to say more and turned to continue over the bridge. He thought of what Janice had said and it dawned on him that, by wrapping Carole in all his attention, he was not letting her overcome her trauma, by keeping her locked into everything she needed to forget. His heart lightened at what Janice was suggesting as he felt like a drowning man being thrown a lifeline.

He walked into the clinic with a lighter eager step and greeted Carole with a robust hug and kissed her as he used to. He felt that she had not shrunk from his embrace and he began to talk to her in a more normal tone. He had been having trouble with the engine of the boat and he embarked on a monologue of engine troubles. He stopped when he realised his line of conversation, but Carole prompted him to continue. He saw that she was engaging with him over his own concerns and seemed to relish the change of topic. He tested her further.

"I bumped into Janice on the bridge. She has returned from Geneva, and I hear, came to see you."

"Yes, surprisingly she did." She said non-committally. Then, "She actually came with a suggestion. An invitation to go to Scotland with her. Don't you think that is absurd." Shaking her head.

Nicholas looked at her and sensed that her denial was not too vehement.

"Do you think so? Well she mentioned it to me and, on reflection, I thought it might actually be good for you. You've seen enough of my craggy old face for the time being, and a change of scene, away from here, might do you good."

She looked at him crestfallen. "You really think so? Of course, I could never have enough of you Nicholas, but perhaps it would allow you to be free for a little while. I have taken up a lot of your time."

He took her hand and kissed it on her palm. "Carole, my darling girl, don't ever think like that, but perhaps a change of scene, away from each other, and this part of the country, might be just what you need. Anyway, it is your decision, and I shall be here for your every wish when you return."

There was nothing in his words that seemed to press her into a decision but she thought she would consider the invitation more fully when he was gone.

****

Janice knocked on the hatchway door and it was opened by Nicholas.

"Permission to come aboard." She shouted briskly.

"Come on in, as you see I have brewed the kettle ready for tea."

She jumped down into the cockpit and looked around the cabin. "My, what a difference, she has certainly been given the luxury treatment, hasn't she? Quite the love-nest I fancy."

He laughed mirthlessly. "Well briefly yes, but I guess I might sell her soon. Too many memories…"

"Thanks." She said as he handed her a mug, "What you need is a different location for her. Is she sea going?"

"Of course, especially since I had a new engine. Although I have just been having trouble with it. But don't you know, she has a noble history, as she was one of the boats that made it to Dunkirk to pick up the British soldiers from the beaches."

'Really, I didn't know that. What a splendid old lady she truly is then."

"Yes, I am very fond of her but I guess Carole will not want to come aboard now!" He said regretfully.

"Oh, she will probably get over things. She loves the water, doesn't she?"

"Yes, we had a marvelous trip up to Bourne End and she is very handy in any situation." He said enthusiastically.

Janice could see that his manner was completely different when he talked of the boat. She had an idea.

"Does your brother like sailing as well?" She asked.

"Well yes, we spent lots of time in our teenage years sailing the Solent, in our summer holidays."

"Perhaps you could motor round to the South Coast and Carole might then be happier to sail it." She paused, she didn't want to make this seem too pre-meditated. She sipped her tea and mentioned the rolls she had purchased.

"I don't suppose you have had much to eat? Well, these will help I think."

He ate gratefully and she could see that, here too, was someone who was looking haggard. She carefully observed his wound and thought it would be much less cruel for him, when it was properly healed but it was obviously a shock for those who were not prepared.

She finished her roll and asked, "Any more tea in the pot?" and they put the kettle on again.

"You know Janice, you have acquired a much more sophisticated air since I last saw you in Geneva, and I would say, if it is not too personal, that you seem to have a special glow about you."

She blushed and looked down. "Hush Nicholas, I suppose you are an expert in such things." She rallied.

"Well, maybe I was." He corrected. "But I am usually aware when someone is unavailable."

She laughed out loud and said. "Indeed, you do Nicholas." In the voice of a Scottish schoolmarm.

Nicholas sat back and looked at her more closely. His voice was altogether lighter in tone to anything she had so far heard and she was glad that he could forget his troubles for a while.

She decided to tease him further. "And I suppose in all your wisdom about the female sex, you can tell who the lucky man is, then?"

"Now that is much too far a leap of intuition Janice, but give me a clue. Is it someone I know?" She laughed again. "Well I suppose that would be telling."

He frowned, "Well, is it someone I know?"

"I'll give you that; It is." She said.

Now she had his attention and they continued the banter and mystery a little longer.

"Don't tell me you are having an illicit affair with Sir Charles." He said outrageously.

She threw him a cushion and continued to tease.

He was silent for some time and said in another voice, raw with emotion. 'Well I know of only two other people of my acquaintance that definitely know you and I hope to God it is not the first." She stopped smiling and bit her lip in vexation. She had brought him back to Georgiou and she swore under her breath.

Damn, I hoped to take his mind off that tack, she thought.

She put her hand on his knee and shook him. "Nicholas, don't think that, I am sorry to tease."

"It is Alex, that I have found, and I hope that he feels the same." And Nicholas whooped with delight.

"The old son of a gun." He exclaimed, "How? When?"

Janice suddenly knew that she must be careful, this was dangerous territory so remarked. "Well actually, we have been exchanging correspondence whilst we have both been away, but I guess now, we can admit our preference."

"Look." She said, as though just thinking about it. Why don't you call Alex, and maybe spend a bit of time together?"

"If Carole decides she wants to come to Scotland, I shall be with her for a week. You and Alex could both catch up on things. Perhaps take the boat to the South Coast, if that were possible." I expect that he is dying to tell you about his time in America.

Nicholas thought and suddenly remembered that he had other responsibilities too, with his father.

"But I must think about my father, I have abandoned him with Tasha and Minka."

She interrupted him. "Don't worry about your father for the time being Nicholas. By all accounts he is fine with them, and is becoming much fitter while walking the downs. Take this time Nicholas to recharge your batteries. She urged him. You may need all your strength." She was silent and he too, each hoping that seeds had been sown.

CHAPTER 9

Time out

Sir Charles was glad to hear of the progress that Carole was making but was taken aback by Janice saying, that she wanted to take Carole away for a while.

"You must remember Sir, that I came back before my annual leave was due, because of the crisis in the House. Well, I can see that this will rumble on and the quickest way to get us all back into action is to let all parties take a break. Parliament is now in recession and perhaps we can all pause for breath." She paused to let it sink in.

"It seems to me, that Carole needs to be in a more normal situation and I thought a week in Scotland, with my parents, might do more to help now, than some fancy clinic in Richmond. You perhaps remember that my father is a doctor, so she will be in safe hands?"

He looked at her and considered what a useful young woman she was proving to be.

He could quite see her logic and it was very much attuned to his own. She also was in the same mold as Ian, and her analytical skills were razor sharp.

"Does this cosy little holiday include Nicholas as well?" He said sardonically.

"Well yes and no, I partly suggested this as a break for him as well. Also, for him to spend time catching up on his own affairs as he seems 'wrung dry' by his concern for Carole."

"I hoped he might take up my suggestion to move his cruiser to Southampton and perhaps catch up with his brother."

"It might also serve your purpose Sir Charles, if he were to check into the office for an up-date on the assignment, and stopped, trying to broach the delicate subject. "I think he is unaware of the 'impasse' on prosecution of the villain Georgiou, and perhaps, it would be better to hear this from you Sir?"

"Em, you may be right. I certainly feel bad about the situation; that once again, this slippery character has got away from our justice system."

"Now. He said briskly, "I have something else for you to cast your eye over Janice, before you disappear. We have just received a report from the CIA, in connection with the new Regime in Cuba. They are really being jumpy about this, as they see a great increase in Soviet activity in that region."

"Fidel Castro has really battened down his country to foreigners and his reforms have sent most of their wealthy landowners and businessmen running to Miami with their cash, for dubious enterprises."

He touched a box on his desk. "I guess this is the last box of 'Havanas' I shall smoke for a while. He said with regret. The reports of increased production of war materials by the Russians, seems to link them to the new Cuban Regime. We have monitored shipping to that region, as have the Americans, and it is definitely hotting up. You can imagine, in the present circumstances of possible leaked documents finding their way to the Russians, that the Americans are hopping mad over the Charlotte Keil Affair. There is bound to be some reference to the American situation and they don't need the Russians to second guess their counter activities."

"Take that Brief away and let me have your comments before you leave? At the week-end I presume?"

"Well, it's not certain but I think that will be about right for us to finalise our arrangements. She confirmed.

That night, Janice rang the clinic and spoke to Carole, who by now had decided to go with her.

Carole had spoken to Nicholas that afternoon and he had told her the news about Alex and Janice and she could see that this contact with the outside world had cheered him up. She saw that he was dying to hear more about his brother's time in America.

After all, she reflected, both men had been away and it was a good opportunity for them to spend time together.

She had seen that something fundamentally had changed in Nicholas with regard to family but she had not questioned him about, it, because they had been engaged in their work, but she could see the affection he had for his adoptive brother.

CHAPTER 10

Scottish Air

Nicholas had collected Carole from the clinic and had travelled with her to London, meeting Janice at Euston Station.

She had said goodbye to Nicholas, rather tearfully, but Janice had bustled her away, to catch the overnight train that was due, so there was no time for second thoughts.

They had travelled to Edinburgh on the night sleeper and had obtained a berth each.

Janice's father had met them at Waverley station, and the short drive to their home, left Carole no time for reflection and she was then met by Janice's mother, who remarked at the newly sophisticated appearance of her daughter. She was also welcomed, by several sisters and dogs.

Carole was amused to see Janice assume a bossy air with them all, being the eldest of all this brood. Her mother was a tall, big boned, curly haired matron, who still showed, that in her youth, she would have been considered 'bonnie.' Her father was just as Carole imagined he would be, with a shock of unruly brown curly hair, greying at the temple, with a long rangy stride, and comfortable tweed jacket, corduroy trousers and stout shoes.

Her mother sported a Murray tartan kilt and almost certainly, Carole thought, a 'Pringle' jumper,' and seemed completely oblivious to passing fashion. These warm sensible clothes had all the attributes of being hard wearing and warm, that every sane person donned when in Scotland, and to Mrs. Murray, was everyday attire.

Carole looked around her bedroom and was drawn to the view that stretched to the mountains across the Firth of Forth.

This country was quite unlike anything she had known and she felt excited for the first time for many days.

She washed her face and hands before joining them all in the family kitchen, where she could smell breakfast frying.

She had been existing on coffee and toast for the past three weeks and the smell of bacon immediately reminded her of her trip up the river but did not bring unpleasant thoughts rushing at her.

Most of the family were gathered around the table in

the middle of a family squabble, and she was not immediately noticed except by Mrs. Murray.

"Girls, girls, stop your arguments, don't forget your manners, we have a guest with us!" She said reprovingly.

Carole smiled and said. "Now tell me your names again, I have got you mixed up I think. Now Janet, you are the elder. Am I right? And Josie, you're next?"

"Yes, but we have a brother in between. He's away at school camp at the moment but he will be back later in the week, worst luck," Josie said in mock gloomy voice.

"I know, sometimes brothers can be a real nuisance, but you wouldn't want to be without them, would you?

"I suppose not." Said Janet grudgingly.

"I had a brother too, but now I regret all the times I fell out with him and felt like you, for he died in a car crash, and I never got to tell him how much I really valued him."

"Oh, how awful." Said Josie. "I didn't really mean it. Wasn't that awful. She said again and took Carole by the hand. Feeling she had transgressed by her unkind remark, she said. "When we've had breakfast, would you like to see my pony? I always go to talk to her when I feel sad."

Carole laughed, "Well, I don't think I could feel sad for too long in this household."

234

"Now children, leave Carole to eat her breakfast. Remember you have finished yours." And Carole was presented with a Scottish version, three times bigger than her usual portion, and she remembered again the trip up the Thames and the breakfast that Ian cooked for Nicholas and herself and felt cheered by the reflection, without the usual clutch at her heart, as she recollected other things. She began to enjoy all the chatter of the children, and Janice wanted to know all their news. "How is your music coming along Josie? Are you still keeping up your practice?"

"Oh yes, and I have joined the school choir. I enjoy that more as, I can sing with other people, instead of doing something on my own."

"But aren't you in the orchestra? Isn't that with other people?"

"Yes." She said slowly. "But I don't like people just looking at me."

"I know how you feel Josie. I didn't like to have people take a lot of notice of me. I just wanted to curl up and hide." Said Carole and Janice realised this was how she had been feeling.

"Now." Janice said. "Run along you two chatterboxes. We have to unpack. There might even be something in my bags for you, but we might take a picnic up to the craggie with your pony if the weather holds."

Day by day Carole joined in the simple pleasures that the family enjoyed and Janice did not pry. To her mother, she had said, only that Carole had been ill, but not to ask questions. She had said something of the matter to her father and he had grunted approval of her actions. "Fresh air, good food and undemanding company will do more good than all this modern psychobabble." He said.

****

Later in the week, Janice proposed a trip into Edinburgh and Carole seemed perfectly happy to go. They caught the train along the valley and were soon in the City. They saw the museum and walked up to the old Citadel overlooking the four corners of surrounding hillsides. Along Princes Street, there were shops and cafés and they stopped to watch the many tourist go by. Here, Janice hoped to confess the part she had played in Geneva.

"Well Carole," Janice began, "do you think this was a good idea?"

"Oh, definitely Janice, I feel much better already. You have a lovely family and I can quite see why you are good at organizing. You must have had many years practice with this tribe. I hope I shall meet your brother too."

"Oh yes, you won't get away without that, Carole. He will breeze in tomorrow and you will hear nothing except his exploits."

"I expect you are both alike as I can see that there is competition there."

"I suppose there is, but most of all, think I get cross when he doesn't use his talents, which are many. He can be easily distracted from the most important things."

"That definitely isn't you!" Carole laughed.

Janice looked at her and was silent for a moment. "Actually, I may have taken that responsibility a bit too seriously, as I have a confession to make, about your visit to Geneva."

Carole looked at her in surprise "Why Janice. that is a very intriguing thing to say. Whatever did you do?"

Janice hesitated but felt that she must be honest, if they were to keep their friendship, for at some time, the facts might turn up.

'Well, I had more than a passing interest in the success of Nicholas's journey to Russia."

"Well, yes I guessed that Janice."

"As part of his journey, has he told you that he was in Geneva?"

"We didn't speak of his trip, no."

"We had to visit Geneva first, to arrange various

details of his journey, which I am not at liberty to tell you about, but," Carole interrupted.

"Hang on, did you say...in December?" Janice nodded and allowed Carole to do the mathematics. "But that means it must have been late in the month?"

"You're right Carole, and indeed he was there when you came to see me."

"I knew it, I knew it." She exclaimed, "Janice what did you do!"

"Well, you must realise, that my job involved seeing to the successful outcome of his venture, and I rather took it into my own hands to make sure he was not distracted from his task." There was silence now as the implications of her confession sank in.

"You mean," Carole said slowly. "that it really was Nicholas that I saw at the hotel? That he really did see me?"

"Yes." Janice said looking at her straight in the face. "On his part, there was no question of him speaking to you. as he was acting under strict orders to a very carefully timed exit, to throw a certain person off his tail. Our return that day was as carefully choreographed, to add distraction, not for Nicholas, but the man who was tailing him but who, had his eyes on you."

"You mean I was used in your plans also?"

"Eventually, yes, but for the rest of the week I was opening and shutting doors so that you should not meet."

"Janice, how could you!" Carole exclaimed.

"With great difficulty, my dear." Said Janice and she put her hand on her friend's arm. "I did it for the success of the venture, but I did it for you both also. If you had seen him earlier in the week, you would have found him in a very confused state, over your part in the arrangements. He was feeling very guilty and it was clear that he regretted having involved you and might even have abandoned his mission, if you had clicked your fingers."

"You mean, he talked to you about me?"

"A little. He asked me to be your friend, and he also asked me to be his friend, and that is what I am striving to be. But I didn't want you to remain in ignorance of my part in things. I truly thought that I could best help you both, by managing things in Geneva."

Carole was silent while she digested what Janice was saying. How could she, what right had she? She fumed, but had to admit that it was too soon, at that moment in Geneva, to know how she would have treated Nicholas. Would anger have beaten forgiveness at that moment? When she thought honestly about her feelings at that time, she admitted that anger might have won and she would never have seen him again. Janice, nanny Janice, damn it, she was probably right.

She also saw that her friend had taken charge of her again, by bringing her to Scotland.

"Janice, at last you are showing your true colours!" Carole shook her head ruefully. "I see I am to be one of your charges for, once again, you are managing me, aren't you?" She said mildly.

Janice breathed more easily, seeing she was forgiven. "Yes, my dear, I suppose I am, and hope sincerely that my darling Alex is doing the same for Nicholas by having a bit of brotherly bonding."

"What! Janice did I hear you right?"

"Yes, my dear, you did." And she got up from the table, having paid the bill, and refused any more discussion for the time being. Janice knew, that the longer Carole was kept from all the details of her own love-life, the less she would dwell on her own recent troubles.

CHAPTER 11

Confessions Time

The visit to Carole by Janice, had come at the moment that Nicholas was at his wits end. Although Carole was definitely better, he felt she was beyond his reach. If only she would decide to go with Janice to Scotland he felt that some of the weight would lift from his shoulders. It had come as a shock to be told that he might even be impeding her recovery! He was at first, hurt by the suggestion, but began to think that perhaps he was too involved to give her any rational perspective on it.

He had certainly considered that she had been grossly violated, but perhaps needed to see this in a more worldly way. He indeed, had to re-evaluate his own life after shocking revelations, but the world didn't really care. It was his ability to adjust that had saved him, and so it must be for her. If only she would take up Janice's offer.

He tossed and turned that night, and in the morning, decided to urge the invitation on her. As he sat watching the sun come up over the river and the geese flying low in their V formation, he remembered his time as a teenager with his brother Alex. The news that Janice had let slip made him suddenly curious and the prospect of a week's catch up with Alex, seemed very appealing! At last he began to look forward to the future instead of the blackness that had threatened him.

Nicholas finally telephoned to his family in Hampshire and there was much relief all round. Tasha and Minka were particularly relieved as they had been aware of something being wrong, at the Bastille Celebrations. Tasha had seen the two river police march someone away down to the river and away by patrol boat. He had seen nothing of either Nicholas or Carole later in the day, and feared that they had been connected to the disturbance, but in what way, he couldn't begin to divine.

Nicholas asked after his father, but in such a distracted voice that even his reassurances of good health didn't convince Tasha that Nicholas was listening. Could he speak to Alex, he asked, and they had duly arranged to meet in London the following day. Perhaps Alex would like a trip down river for a few days with him. Tasha nodded furiously when he heard this request and so Alex was dispatched to hear his brother's news.

He found Nicholas at Richmond tinkering with his engine. He emerged as he heard a familiar voice.

"Ahoy there, anyone on board?" And a deeply tanned giant stood on the pontoon.

"Alex, come on board. You are just the man I need. I have engine trouble and all our plans will go nowhere, if it isn't fixed."

He jumped on board and embraced Nicholas then holding his shoulders he looked at his brother candidly.

"My God, Nico, what have they done to you." He said with the frankness of brotherhood.

Nicholas laughed. "That's Alex, straight to the point, no pulling punches, eh?"

Alex continued to stare. "Well, it will look better when the scar heals, but it must have been a very nasty blow, and you must tell me how you got it. But for now, I reckon you want my help with that engine." As his father's son, he knew when to take charge and fix things.

They worked on the engine and, by the time Alex had investigated, there were several pieces of engine parts on the seats. With care, and plenty of engine oil, the mechanics were working perfectly by the time the sun was 'over the yardarm' and they made tracks to the nearest Public House. They entered a Georgian bay windowed hostelry overlooking the river, and ordered two well-deserved pints of Youngs Best Bitter and a 'ploughmans' satisfied their hunger. In a state of pleasant euphoria, they sat back and appraised each other after their six months away in opposite directions in the world.

Each saw the change in the other, which was to a marked degree. Alex began to speak but Nicholas interrupted him.

"Well you've certainly done some growing up since last I saw you Alex."

"Well it has been a wonderful experience, riding and roping the horses. There was a lot of hard work and hard riding involved and I had to handle my fair share of farm machinery whilst I was there. You have no idea how large these are. They are perfectly suited to the jobs they have to do because everything is so vast over there, and the acreage involved, is enormous. I felt quite hemmed in, when I arrived home."

"Well you've filled out a lot since I saw you last. Worked up some good muscles from what I can see. Quite a hit with the Texan girls I've no wonder?"

"As a matter of fact, Nicholas, it should have been you there. at all the hoedowns. There were lots of eager young women but to tell the truth, they frightened the life out of me. You, now, would have been in your element. You would have sweet talked the lot of them." Looking at his brother in admiration on this front.

"That's as maybe in the past but hardly a pretty sight now, hey?"

"Well no." Said Alex frankly. "But to tell the truth, I

think you will find that the girls might just go for that savage pirate look Nicholas shook his head but said nothing. They sat in companionable silence knowing there was much to say between them, but with leisure to catch up on events.

Nicholas could feel his pre-occupation falling from his shoulders and he was content to feel the sun on his face. It was, as Janice had suggested, a time to stand back from all of his commitments and he refrained from asking any more questions.

The bees hummed and the swallows turned and wheeled around the rooftops of the buildings, darting into the eaves to feed their young. But Nicholas was beyond seeing their frantic swooping and catching of flies over the river. The lunchtime crowd had returned to work and he and Alex sat contentedly in a blue haze as they smoked their cigarettes.

****

They returned to the cruiser late in the afternoon with armfuls of provisions and bottles of beer and whisky. They intended to use the riverside pubs at lunchtime but were content to spend the rest of the time on board.

"This is a bit more luxurious since I last saw her." Said Alex, "Quite a love-nest, eh!"

Nicholas grunted but said no more. His blanket of

despair enclosed him again and Alex could have bitten off his tongue at his silly remark.

They made their way down river and anchored up at Kingston. By now, Nicholas had regained his composure and was happy to be occupied with steering the boat down river. The nights were still relatively light, especially on the river, with the reflections of lamps on land, but a sharp wind had sprung up and promised rain for the next day.

They made fast securely, as the night might prove to be stormy and battened down all their equipment.

Alex was very impressed with the new engine and wanted to know all the details. "This engine has a remarkable specification Nicholas. Why do you need such power and how about those electronics and radio transmitters?"

"Well I guess that's how things are going now. I just thought it would make the old lady a bit more seaworthy. Do you fancy taking her round to Portsmouth?"

"Well she's certainly more fit for it than she was. Let's see how tomorrow's weather holds. I don't fancy trying my chances if the weather deteriorates."

"Now, are you ready for a T-bone steak like we had in Texas?" Alex finally asked.

"Sure do, partner." Said Nicholas in mock cowboy

speak, having grown up on John Wayne films. Steak and ale replete, they poured themselves whiskies and lit their cigarettes and out of the under-bunk cupboard, Nicholas produced some cards. Soon the cabin resembled the saloon bar of their favourite movie. Alex sensed that Nicholas was happy not to talk for the time being, and he plied him with more whisky to ensure a forgetful night.

He could see that Nicholas had a very troubled mind, and had been truly shocked at his appearance. It was as if he had aged ten years in the last six months and Alex was clearly at a loss how to help him. They settled down to some serious card playing and went to bed drunk as skunks.

The wind howled and they didn't hear it.

The rain squalled and it disturbed them not

The boat rocked and skewed and they slept on.

Dawn broke grey and uninviting but they knew it not and the rest of London was fully awake and roaring before there was any sign of life on board.

Visits to the heads was the main priority and by 11 o'clock all sense of feminine presence was completely erased by their smoke filled, alcoholic and farting male dominance.

They both woke to an excruciatingly thick head and no conversation. Black coffee and a cigarette were their companions, and all sense of pride in appearance had left them…but it felt bloody good.

Meanwhile, the rain beat down and the wind howled and there was nothing more attractive than some more sleep.

****

In Scotland Carole was hearing the bare bones of Janice's love life.

"We have been writing to each other all the time we have been away and I guess, we both felt the same way about things, when we met a couple of weeks ago."

Carole prompted her. "You mean just like that, no romantic dinner or what?"

"Of course, you silly, we went to the West End and saw 'West Side Story'. Marvelous, Alex was just as sentimental as I was, and it just set us off. You know I'm not back at the Kensington flat now but in Belgravia. It just seemed the right moment with the right man."

"I know what you mean." Said Carole dreamily. "That's how I felt about Nicholas. The right moment with the right man, even though I knew he would leave me, that he would betray me." She paused. "Did you know that was the plan Janice?"

"I guess so, Carole, but I don't think he ever intended to hurt you, I think no-one was more surprised than he was, that he had fallen into the trap of loving you and, having to live with the knowledge that he had used you." She continued, "But, he did get a second chance, didn't he? And you did forgive him, didn't you?"

Carole was silently sobbing.

Janice turned her round and let her sob on her shoulder. When she had stopped her tears, Janice repeated her question. "But you did give him a second chance, didn't you? So why do you think he can't forget this 'other thing?'"

With muffled voice Carole said. "Oh, I do hope so, I do hope so." And they sat there with Janice stroking her friend's hair.

This marked a turning point for Carole and she then entered into the lives of the children with enthusiasm, even riding Janet's pony and swimming in the river pools, stripped naked like everyone else.

****

In London, the rain had finally stopped by the evening and the two reprobates had their appetites back again. Some semblance of masculine pride returned and a good shake out of cabin and bedding was undertaken. A shave seemed more than they could muster but at least they had use of the shower and smartened up enough to take themselves off to the pub. They ordered pie and chips and the local brew, but

249

this time they kept their drinking moderate as their excesses were still giving them headaches.

There was a group of musicians to entertain them and there was no need for conversation there for a while. Later Nicholas ribbed Alex about his budding romance.

"Now Alex, I see you are a new man and have all the vices of the rest of us. What about romance? I met Janice, you remember Janice don't you, your partner at the Arts Ball, and she tells me,"

"What does she tell you." Interrupted Alex growling

"Well, actually she didn't need to tell me that she was unavailable. You see, I know these things."

Alex said hotly. "Well how did you know about us?"

Nicholas laughed and laughed and Alex realised that he had been fooled into admitting their liaison.

"I didn't, but I see that I was right. Well, Alex, I guess you are not the kind to fool around like me, so may I take it that this romance is serious? For, in my opinion, for what it is worth, you grab her with both hands and don't let her go. She is a canny 'wee lassie' and I have great respect for her judgment. She has been a great friend to me in the past so, you certainly have my approval."

"What do you mean, she has been? She wasn't?" He stopped in confusion.

"No, no." Nicholas hastily reassured him, "Just a professional relationship but I value her opinions."

At that Alex agreed, especially as it dawned on him that Janice had probably been instrumental in setting up this time with his brother.

CHAPTER 12

Limitations of the Law

Sir Charles arrived at Whitehall early. His indigestion was keeping him awake at night so he was up earlier than usual. He had walked from Waterloo over Westminster Bridge hoping to clear his head. The watery sun was rising in the east and he would have liked to linger. The air was fresh after the rain and the pavements were washed clean but the tide of humanity carried him across the bridge and up Whitehall towards Trafalgar Square. He passed by the flotsam of humanity, sleeping in the doorways and alleys, near the river, but he did not see them. His concern was to keep humanity from blowing itself up in global conflict and that danger seemed very real to him this lovely summer morning.

There was to be a demonstration later by a new movement called CND, who were foolishly thinking they could bring both parties, in this Nuclear game of 'Moriarty,' to put their weapons down and come to the table. How wrong they were. He thought angrily, as he grappled with preventing Nuclear War. Neither side of the Iron Curtain would trust the other, to lay down their arsenal of Nuclear Warheads. What did these 'crackpots' think they could do to change the minds of Heads of State.

His anger rose and so did his prospects for another night of dyspepsia.

He was expecting a busy day. He had first to see Mr. Nicholas Baron, and then the Prime Minister, and if he was lucky, or perhaps unlucky, taking into account his state of health, a late lunch with Buzz Berkeley Redfern in Pall Mall.

****

Nicholas had told Alex that he had some business to conduct in Westminster and agreed to meet at The Tate for lunch. There was a Picasso Exhibition running and he had not yet had time to view. He expected to be with Sir Charles for a short while, so there was plenty of the day to spend motoring down river.

He moored up at his old berth in Chelsea and left his brother there to walk along the Embankment.

He was in no hurry as he was early for his appointment. He enjoyed watching the craft on the river. They distracted him from thinking about the meeting with his boss.

He had thought that Sir Charles wanted to see him about the Bastille Celebrations and he had steeled himself to be professional about the outcome. He was, however, not looking forward to re-opening fresh wounds.

He entered the office from Whitehall and was shown up to Sir Charles room.

"Ah, good morning Mr. Baron, good to see you, extending his hand. Do draw up a seat, is it a Sobranie today?" And he extended his box of assorted cigarettes to Nicholas, with a smile.

"Definitely not. Actually, I think I would most prefer a Players Navy Cut, but I guess you don't smoke such ordinary kind?

"Actually Nicholas," He said less formally. "We cater for all tastes. After all, we are mostly military men here, and habits acquired in youth are hard to break." And he reached to find another box in his side drawer.

This time there was no irony in his words but a man trying to put his guest at ease. He did not hurry the moment, because he knew that the news he had to impart would not be welcome. He produced a lighter to ignite the proffered cigarette, returning to his own Navy Cut to light his own.

"I heard from Janice this morning that her guest is well and enjoying the Scottish air. I believe she is helping to organize three younger siblings of the family, and is being kept well occupied."

Nicholas held on to his words and felt some of the tension leave him. Sir Charles took a leisurely puff on his cigarette and was silent for a while. Then he said.

"Here, I am afraid, the news is not so good. The Russian Embassy is up to its old tricks and have claimed diplomatic immunity for our 'guest' in H.M. Prisons."

There was a sharp intake of breath as Nicholas realised that Georgiou had wriggled free again. His sense of justice was outraged and he clenched his fist.

"That can't be so, tell me he can't get away with it, why, I saw with my own eyes…" He halted and put his head in his hands.

"Yes, that was cruel." Said Sir Charles gently. "But then, I imagine that was exactly what he wanted, and one day we will have to deal with him. But perhaps you have not thought through the consequences of bringing him to justice?"

He paused, as Nicholas still held his head bowed.

"If we had been able to prosecute his crime, we would have laid Carole open to a very public scrutiny of the events and, make no mistake, the Russians would have got the best lawyers to discredit her evidence, regardless of truth. Do you really want that for her?"

"Well, no, of course not, I have not been thinking that far, just that he must be punished." He said fiercely.

He was silent for a minute and then Sir Charles said. "In this business, there are many ugly deeds, and the only way to survive, is to stay true to your belief in the justice of your cause, and the love we bear our families. War, by any means, is the ugliest manifestation of man's nature and we are called upon to administer that justice in our own way. We do our job to prevent what we see as another catastrophe."

He went on. "You have been an enormous help in keeping the peace and exploring the darker side of national defence. Carole has also been trained in that too, so she should be better prepared to accept the consequences. All we can do to chase away the shadows from our own lives, is to find some forgiveness in our hearts and accept the consequences."

After a pause, he continued "Nothing and no-one is perfect in this life, and we have to learn to accept that, for I rather think you are taking too much onto your own shoulders, in this matter. Just live and love one another, is my advice to you both."

The silence that followed his words stretched onwards. The ash on his cigarette lengthened but he did not attempt to remove it. He watched the young man in all his turmoil until the clock on Big Ben again recalled him to himself and Nicholas stood up.

They shook hands and Nicholas said, "Thank you Sir." And left the office quickly as he felt a rising tide of bile overtake him and he retched into the gutter. 'Who was he to judge Georgiou, had he also not signed up to use Carole, was he not guilty of the same crime? Dear God, I hope not." He cried in abandonment.

****

Alex, waiting on the Embankment, could see that Nicholas was walking towards him like a drunken man and was alarmed. He rushed towards Nicholas and was assailed by the acrid smell of bile and knew this man was unwell. He could not understand what had overtaken Nicholas but helped him to walk the rest of the way to the boat.

By this time Nicholas was shivering violently despite the summer warmth. Alex helped him onto the pontoon and into the boat where Nicholas fell onto the bed in a state of collapse. His brother covered him up with blankets and put on a kettle to make him some sweet tea and forced him to drink it and eat a small piece of bread. Despite the blanket, his teeth chattered and his shoulders shook.

Alex sat by his side and rubbed his shoulders and back and gradually the shivering gave way to loud sobs.

Alex was astonished but continued to hold his brother in his arms. What on earth had happened, he wondered, but held the man steadily in his grip. At last sleep had come and Alex left him covered, with all the blankets he could muster, and went back to the galley.

He made a cup of tea for himself and took it into the cockpit. He stood somberly looking across the water and began to conjecture what Nicholas had experienced while away in Eastern Europe and felt that this was the key to his collapse. The experience that his father Stefan had hinted of, came back to him, and he wondered whether this was at the heart of the matter.

****

It was well into the afternoon before Nicholas woke and he wondered why he was here in his bunk, then he remembered and he groaned.

Alex heard him stir and looked in on him. "Ah, you're awake brother. Are you feeling any better? Can I get you a drink, water?"

Nicholas nodded and closed his eyes again. He now felt rested and didn't seem to have anything wrong. What on earth had happened to him?

Alex returned with a drink of water and looked appraisingly at Nicholas.

"Well that was a nasty turn, Nicholas, I think it looked like shock, as you don't seem to have anything wrong now."

"I don't know whether I should really pry but it seems to me you have not recovered from your injury and whatever it was that caused it, and maybe you need to unburden yourself to someone who cares?"

"Oh, that's not all of it, believe me." Nicholas managed. "I don't know that I really can tell you everything, but some at least partly concerns you."

Alex said gravely. "Try me."

Nicholas tried to marshal his thoughts, which seemed to be playing tricks with him.

Alex prompted. "Well, tell me about the horses and your time in Siberia."

"Oh that. Well the main reason I was able to achieve that goal was because I went back to our family farm at least it was, but is now under the control of the Government, but has been run by my uncle as if it was his own. The Government doesn't intervene as long as they get their quota of dray horses."

"My Uncle Dimitri has a son named Mikhail who has a passionate love of the horses and is a very good horse breeder, as was my uncle. I was partly raised by my Aunt Babeta and Uncle Dimitri, so my love and knowledge of horses started there, on the farm. My mother was always delicate and didn't take to country life, so my father lived with her in Moscow. At that time, he was a professor of Naval Engineering. Times changed and he lost his job at the University because he was considered a bad influence on the students, a radical. He returned to the farm and wrote the book that caused his banishment to Siberia as a dissident. Most of the history you now know but what I had forgotten was the visceral dislike that Mikhail harboured towards me – indeed it was mutual, but I tried to master it, because I needed their help to take the horses to sell in Siberia." He stopped, this had already taken much of his strength.

Alex waited.

"All my plans to rescue my father were successful, too successful in fact, as the horse trading we had negotiated, had set Mikhail on fire to do some more travelling. There seemed to be a longstanding feud with his father about leaving the farm, as Stefan had done in his youth when he had joined the Navy."

"This disagreement bubbled under the surface, all the way we travelled on the train to the harbour." He stopped again to collect his thoughts. "As part of my bargain with them, I renounced any claim to the farm, if it ever became theirs officially again, and this had been Uncle Dimitri's heart's desire. Then, when Mikhail talked of leaving, his frustration spilled over when we reached the Port."

"Beside my renunciation of the farm, we had also to get Stefan's consent. I had thought it would be automatic. Somehow the argument became so heated that Mikhail pulled a knife. I didn't understand all the undercurrents of the argument but, at some point, it became clear that Mikhail was not my cousin, but my half-brother." Alex gasped. "And what was worse, when I intervened to try to stop the recriminations between Uncle Dimitri and Mikhail, he struck out at me, giving me this wound and what was even worse, struck his own father/stepfather in the back."

"At this, Stefan, instead of acknowledging his newly revealed son's claim to the farm, renounced him as his heir, because he said that Mikhail bore evidence of all the worst excesses in his own nature, and he disowned him, as a treacherous human being, who had struck (mortally or otherwise) his legal father. By this time, I was unable to do anything to help anyone, and I was hurried onto the ship with Stefan and left them awaiting an ambulance. I still do not know what the outcome was."

Alex was silent when he had heard this tale. He began to appreciate the turmoil that this family argument, had left Nicholas in. He was puzzled by what had happened to Nicholas at that point.

"How did you make it to the ship in your state?"

"I had arranged with the corn merchant to supply fodder for the horses and he was witness to what had happened and, with remarkable presence of mind, helped me to board. He was also due to embark, and made sure, that I received immediate treatment. He also called for an ambulance for Dimitri but did not wait its arrival, as the ship was leaving. He only knew, that Dimitri was still alive when we left. and hoped that medical assistance would arrive timely."

"The Captain was used to quayside disputes with his own crew, and was anxious to depart, so that no questions were asked by the Port Authorities, and he hightailed it out of Leningrad."

"A Corn Merchants agent, did you say? He sounds a pretty useful guy to have around. He also saw to things at the other end?" Alex by now, was incredulous at the chain of events, but thought it best to let that lie for the time being. It was enough to hear of the emotional overload of the events.

"Well, in the circumstances, I think you were damned lucky to make it home."

"Yes, I was, I know, but I have felt so uncertain of my convictions and motives for everything. I feel I have to question why I acted like I did in the first place. I was pretty cold blooded in taking on the project. After all, I preyed on an innocent girl, we preyed on two innocent girls, to help us in our endeavours. Yes, we have both fallen in love with them and think everything is fine. But it is not; because I am worse than a rapist in my cold-blooded usage of Carole."

"I didn't see it before, I thought it was just because I was not looking out for her, but now I know I am no better than that monster Georgiou."

"What are you saying, Nicholas, you're not making sense? What has Georgiou got to do with it?"

Nicholas shook his head and put his hands over his face and was silent.

Alex looked at him and thought better about pressing him. Things were looking dark indeed and he was not sure he should hear any more, but he pondered the part he had played in setting up the exchange and agreed that it had not been just a bit of fun.

He put his hand on Nicholas's shoulder and said lightly. "I guess you have had quite enough for one day, I'm going to get some food for us. I'll be back soon, if you can get the cabin organized." He said as he jumped onto the pontoon and headed for the 'chippy.'

CHAPTER 13

Reunion

The week passed all too quickly for the friends, but by the end of it, Carole had a special place in her heart for this wild and open landscape. She had been used to the hills of Wales during all her childhood, but here the scale was magnified and had a grandeur which, she thought, far surpassed her knowledge of the Welsh mountains. They had walked, and ridden and swum, and visited the city and port, and had hardly touched upon her own problems.

Here she had been free to think about her experiences, and to put them into the context of a whole life. She was able to rationalise what was most important to her, and how she achieved it.

She knew that Nicholas loved her, but they had both been engaged in a dangerous business. She had known this when Nicholas came home from Europe, scarred in mind and body.

She had been trained in defensive techniques so knew some of the risks that might be involved. They had certainly known that Georgiou was dangerous, and that he wanted 'blood.' But she had knowingly, put herself beyond the protective cordon, that had been placed around them. So, she must face the responsibility for her own actions, in giving Georgiou an opportunity to hurt Nicholas, through her. *But despite these actions they were still alive and able to love each other, weren't they? She must show Nicholas that she could do this.*

The weekend arrived and she and Janice packed their bags.

"You will come to see us again." Said Janet, who had been Carole's shadow all week. "My pony will be sorry you are leaving us."

"And so, will I, Janet. I shall be sorry to leave you too, but I will keep you in my heart and maybe you can come and visit me in London one day and we can show you the special places to see in the capital. There are many beautiful parks and the river is endlessly changing. It is not all dirt and smoke stacks. There are palaces and museums full of strange things. In the heart of the city, are strange markets and people from every part of the world that have made their home there.

"I don't know whether I want to go to such a big place. I won't know anyone there."

Carole looked at her and said. "It is certainly a big place and it does take time to adjust, but it is wonderful to visit and your big sister would be there."

With that, the child had to be content. Carole sighed. She had loved being with Janice's family and she was reminded of how much she missed her dead brother, for somehow, family life had never been the same after the car accident.

"Come on Carole, we shall miss our train if we don't get moving." Janice reminded her and they hurried to pile their cases in her father's car.

"Goodbye Mrs. Murray, thank you for making me so welcome."

"I hope you come again wee hen, we have enjoyed your company." And with a wave she was on her way home, with all her resolve strengthened by this visit.

CHAPTER 14

Manipulated by a Wee Scottish Lassie

The next morning the brothers had risen early and were headed down river before the commuters arrived in their droves. They had passed London Bridge, and were heading for Greenwich before they had eaten breakfast, and planned to anchor up beyond the docks, near Gravesend.

They had to keep their eyes sharp, as the merchant shipping was very busy and needed to be avoided, every sea mile they travelled. Nicholas pointed out the different docks and the cargoes that came to each one. All the derricks were hard at work discharging all the goods and the lighters were like bees around a hive, taking off goods for discharge further upstream. Barges pulled the larger ships into their docking points and all was bustle and noise.

Once again, they passed Greenwich and Alex was as enraptured as Carole had been, to see the Cutty Sark in all her glory, At the next bend, the river opened up wider and left behind the incessant activity of the docks. Here the marshes could be seen, stretching away ahead of them and the buildings, warehouses and factories fell away on both sides, for a while.

At last they came to the small pontoon where Nicholas had moored with Carole, and he steered the boat into the bank with sure hands. Alex was ready to jump overboard and they anchored up with the same seamanship that Carole had shown.

"That was fantastic Nicholas," Alex said enthusiastically. "What a wonderful part of the river. We have no idea of the grandeur of London until you see it from the water."

"I agree. That's partly why I brought you down here."

They secured the boat and put on the kettle. It was not long before a fried breakfast was ready and they satisfied their hunger.

Alex then asked. "You said that this spot is partly why you brought me here. What other reason did you have?"

"Well I thought you might like to see where my adventures began."

He pointed to the opposite bank. "That's where I was met by Georgiou and his friend who intended to take the pearls from me."

"What the devil?" Alex exclaimed.

"Yes, you may well be surprised. I had been approached by Georgiou after the death of Boris who knew about the Chevaliers' plan for the pearls. God knows how they found out, but he had tried to blackmail me about them by threatening to expose the whole plot to his father, the Attaché. He and Boris had cooked up a plan to steal them under our eyes and sell them in England and pocket the money for themselves."

"They knew that the Chevaliers were trying to smuggle them abroad without any of the Authorities knowing, and he reckoned he could steal them with impunity since officially they didn't exist."

"Somehow MI5 got wind of what was happening and, in return for unofficially helping me take the pearls out of the country, I was to help them with one or two things whilst away. Like the Chevaliers, they considered my father …my father…a valuable 'asset' and were happy to help in our endeavours."

"You mean, you were recruited as a 'spy?" Alex asked, amazed.

"If you want to call it that, yes. I guess I didn't then realise how fundamental that commitment was, but I soon found out."

"Oh Nicholas, you were really going in deep. There was I thinking we were on a 'jolly' whilst you had problems of a quite different kind. Yes, that Georgiou was always a boastful brute of a man and hung around with a very dubious crowd in the East End Gym he frequented." Said Alex.

"I was recruited to persist with the plan to steal the pearls from Carole only they had gone missing. Up in Whitehall they instructed me to carry out my original plan and they would make sure the pearls were forthcoming."

"It seemed that Carole had found out that they were not fake and, in panic, had hidden them from us all, when she realised that Boris had drunk a glass of alcohol meant for her, and had promptly dropped down dead."

"She knew that this was a serious situation but did not know who to trust. All my charm and deviousness would have got me nowhere, if she had not been enlisted, through Janet, to her boss's plan and was told to give me the pearls. In every other respect she knew nothing, but was made aware of my perfidy when I left her...when I left her consummate in the boat." Nicholas looked straight at his brother and took in the full horror of his reaction. "Yes, it was utter betrayal of someone I later realised, I loved. She gave them to me perfectly willingly and, at that moment, she gave herself to me knowing full well I would take them and go, perhaps never to return."

They were both silent while Alex digested this.

"Well it certainly didn't put you in a good light. I wonder that she took you back on your return. She did take you back by all accounts?"

Nicholas said bleakly. "Yes, and there's the pity of it,

I'm her nemesis, don't you see. For she has been made to suffer for me.

Alex was afraid to ask and held his breath.

"God help me, I might just as soon have raped her myself and gone off with the pearls in my selfishness, but no, in my arrogance, I had to return and make her pay for my duplicity, for that was what it was. I managed to get away from Georgiou by a pre-determined snatch by the river police. At the same time, I flung myself over the sided of the boat I was using, to pass the pearls over to Georgiou. He, and his friend from his East End gym were taken into custody over our 'plan.'

He had thought that I had drowned and that the pearls were lost in Thames mud. However, it was a ruse, for I was picked up further down the river by a pre-arranged cutter who took me to 'The Ice Maiden' which was to take me to Copenhagen. And then I was on my way east.

Six months later, Georgiou, who thought that I was dead, saw us both together and realised that he had been duped. Carole was then targeted by him, to make me pay."

Alex was speechless at the admission Nicholas had made. In all honesty, he could only agree with Nicholas' analysis and it appalled him. He was aware, that he had taken on the role of confessor, and that Nicholas was seeking forgiveness. But, how could he? How should he? He was not the injured party here.

271

"Have you asked Carole about this? How does she regard you now?"

Nicholas steadied himself. "Well she doesn't reject me, she will see me. But for several weeks, she has been in a clinic in a state of breakdown and I don't know how to reach her. She has been in another world Alex, and I am afraid, oh so afraid." His voice broke and he could say no more.

Alex in a more perceptive moment said, "Then why are you here and not at her side?"

"You might well ask! But after three weeks of visiting her every day, I had an unofficial visit from Janice, who knew the state of affairs through official channels. I'll say no more of that, except that she offered me a lifeline, I suppose."

"She has taken Carole to Scotland for a week and somewhere along the conversation we had when she visited me, at Richmond, suggested I contact the family, you in particular, I think she said, and of course I now know why, for you have both taken on the role of guardian angels"

Alex laughed and the conversation lightened, "Oh, I don't know about that, I'm no guardian angel, but I fancy that Janice knows exactly what she is doing in giving you both time for a little reflection. I am beginning to believe I have taken on a formidable young lady who will twist me round her little finger before I have said. 'Jack Rabbit'."

At last Nicholas too, laughed, and reflected that yes, one way or another, their destiny was controlled by the fairer sex.

For the rest of the holiday no more was said of the past but they enjoyed exploring the lower reaches of the Thames. They stopped at wayside pubs and anchored up finally, at Chatham where they saw all the history of this island in the fully functioning shipyard there. They were fascinated by all things mechanical and nautical, and needed no second bidding to explore onboard, some of the ships anchored there. Alex was adept at talking with technical interest and in all such things men love to show off their current toys, and they were invited into the bowels, the beating heart of these monsters of the sea.

By the time they returned to their anchorage at Chelsea they were both relaxed and infinitely glad of this chance moment, in their lives.

They were due to meet the girls at Janice's flat. Alex had come to London in his MG and suggested Nicholas borrow it for some time away with Carole, and he would return home by train.

They rang the bell of the flat and Carole answered the door and Alex stepped through. "Carole, how lovely to see you. My, that Highland air has been good for you, you are as brown as a berry." She blushed and he entered into the main room and swept Janice off her feet, planting a kiss on her mouth and said, "Oh, my darling girl, I have missed you." And swirled her round, as she protested weakly.

"Put me down!" But he only laughed.

Meanwhile Nicholas and Carole looked at each other more uncertainly but he hugged her to him and said into her hair. "Hello, my love, I have missed you."

"And me, you, Nicholas" She whispered.

There were a few more pleasantries exchanged but it was clear that Janice and Alex were anxious to speed them on their way, and they drove swiftly out of London in Alex' MG Sport.

CHAPTER 15

Putting the Past Away

Nicholas was at a loss to know how to help her, but help her he would. He had driven them to a small hotel in the Surrey hills. He smiled encouragingly at her.

"Well, how does this suit you?"

"Oh, Nicholas this is lovely. Perhaps we can go for a walk when we have registered?"

"Of course." He said, relieved to have put off an awkward moment. "The breeze is just soft enough to enjoy." Nicholas took their cases to a room that overlooked fields with horses grazing and away on the opposite hill they could see a church spire.

He hesitated to know how to approach her, as her manner was remote. He took her hand and raised it to his lips, closing his eyes. Then, before she had a chance to withdraw it, He said. "Come on, get those shoes on, as you are going to walk those socks off." He warned lightly.

They took the road to a coppice of trees and she did not remind him of her recent time walking the Scottish Highlands. The pathway led them through the whispering trees, into a meadow beyond. Clouds scudded across the sky as, far above, the sky was streaked with mare's tails and lower cumulus clouds. The swifts were swooping low over the rooftops and Nicholas wondered whether they should have taken raincoats.

He took her hand and she didn't withdraw it. Nicholas did not know how to treat her and was treading on eggshells, indeed he felt that she was enclosed in a carapace and he was afraid to crack the surface.

The trees above them susurrated gently and helped to cover the silence that had descended upon them.

It was mid-afternoon and many of the sounds of life were stilled. It was as though all had eaten well and were dozing in the heat of the day.

They crossed a field of horses with their foals, and a fine chestnut mare looked enquiringly but did not come up to them.

Nicholas held Carole back with his hand and whinnied experimentally at the horse who pricked up her ears. "Don't move." Said Nicholas softly to Carole and whinnied again.

The horse moved forward uncertainly towards them and Nicholas extended his hand towards the mare, who responded with a snort and came closer. Nicholas put out his hand for the horse to nuzzle and to eat the nuts lying there. This gift eaten, the horse nuzzled him again and bent to explore his pockets. All this time he spoke to the mare as he scratched behind her ears and down her lovely neck.

"My, you're bonnie now aren't you my beauty. You see," He said to Carole ruefully. Even mares fall for my charms."

"Of course, why wouldn't they." And she looked at him directly for the first time in one whole month, and his heart sang.

Steady. He thought to himself.

The next moment the mare began to explore around Carole and she stroked her gently on the muzzle, "I'm afraid I haven't anything for you, my lovely." She said in West Country brogue. "I didn't anticipate that you would like some of these nuts." Carole said, talking to the mare. But she will not leave us alone unless she knows we have nothing more for her Nicholas.

"Yes, she's a greedy one but let's leave them to return to the grass." And they turned their backs on the horse and walked slowly to the fence line and over the stile. "You showed no fear there Carole?" He queried.

"No of course not. I was a fully paid up member of the Pony Club." She laughed jokingly and Nicholas was satisfied they had passed a milestone.

"So, you would be happy to ride the Russian horses

of mine?" He asked hesitatingly. She looked at him surprised.

"What do you mean? Are these your horses?" She asked amazed.

"They are indeed, and they hold many memories for me of my time away, but they are still in quarantine and I cannot take them home yet. Papa Tasha and I, intend to breed from them." Carole seemed to be aware of everything around her and more like the woman he had known. She had always responded in lively fashion to any conversation and her silent unresponsiveness of the past month seemed to be falling away.

They came to a lych-gate into a church yard and began to read the tombstones, passing from one to another, marveling at their age and the whole families buried there.

They read the inscriptions on the War Memorial and saw how many family names were repeated on the list. Every village had given sons to the ravages of war and the formal memorials to this fact, were a testimony to their bravery. Whole families of menfolk all seemed to have been sacrificed, and it was with sober thoughts that they entered the small church.

In the porch were Parish Notices and reminders of the Parish Fete and at the back of the church, was the children's corner. In the church tower, ropes were hung with different colours to denote the ring tone.

Carole began to tell him of the wonderful peel of bells in her own town of Avonbridge at the Abbey, and Nicholas could not help but agree, without thinking.

She looked at him oddly. "What do you mean? How do you know what those bells sound like?"

He looked sheepishly down to the ground and wondered whether he should tell her.

"Well, actually I have heard them several times. You certainly need earplugs if you try to sleep through them. I remember one Saturday night tossing and turning to the hourly sound of the bells and couldn't blot out the sound of returning revelers from a midsummer river barbecue. I heard every shushed note of quiet made by them as they came home IN THE EARLY MORNING." He emphasized the last few words and looked at her accusingly.

"Nicholas! What are you saying?" She asked.

"Well, what I am saying is, your parents have some new neighbours."

"Nicholas!" She shrieked. "What are you saying?" She stopped and shook his arm as he laughingly fended her off. He took her hands and enclosed them on his chest whilst taking her into his arms.

"Caro, Caro, don't you know I have been jealously guarding you, until, until. And a sob broke from him and they clung together in silence.

When he recovered sufficiently to carry on, he told her of his house.

"Do you remember that your parents had a new neighbour, and I think, a new cat?"

"Oh Nicholas, so it was our fat tabby from the boat."

"Indeed, it is." He said. "It was the only place I could take it to, when the boat was refitted but it is a vagrant all the same and will find a home wherever it ingratiates itself."

"Yes, indeed it does, and did you know, it suns itself on my bed!"

"Oh, how I wished I had known that. It would have given me great comfort when I watched."

"Did you need great comfort?" She said rather strangely, and he knew that she was touching on more serious matters.

"Yes, I did, for I knew that everything was my fault. It was my willful disregard for your feelings that led me into such selfishness."

"No, no." She shook her head and he felt her tremble.

As they left the church, they were both silent, thinking their own thoughts.

Nicholas steered Carole towards a bench in the

churchyard. And they sat down companionably, seemingly content to remain quiet in these peaceful surroundings.

But soon Nicholas turned towards Carole and took her hand, absentmindedly stroking her palm, until he had gathered his thoughts.

"Caro, dear heart, I wish to say something to you that you should know, and I hope that you will hear me out. My thoughts are still rather chaotic, but hope you will give me time to explain myself."

She put her hand over his and nodded.

Nicholas continued. "You will remember when you first saw me, after I came back from Russia? I was feeling very despondent all round, at that moment. I had spent six months trying to fulfil my mission of bringing my father out of Siberia. When I started on, what I thought of as an adventure, with heroic deeds to complete, I had little thought of the chain of reaction that I would release. Well, that idea pretty quickly proved to be anything but the case."

"First Boris had died, who knows by whose hand. Then the sudden onset of your illness afterwards, brought home to me that you must also be in danger. This had not been my intention when…" he paused, at a loss to explain the plan.

"I was instructed to make friends with a suitable innocent young lady who was to carry the pearls out of

Anna Romaine's apartment. A fake robbery could be supposed to have happened, which would have included the loss of the most valuable Imperial possession, i.e. the pearls. In these stringent times, it is impossible to sell them in England without coming to the notice of the authority that deals with the sale of National Treasures. This would have incurred a probable ban on export. Any money that would have been raised on their sale in England, would again, have been subject to a statutory limit, if this was to be taken out of the country. So, a sale of the pearls in Switzerland seemed a good idea, but must be taken out of the country by subterfuge."

"The pearls were freely given by Anna Romaine because she believed in the return of Imperial Rule and she wanted to further this cause through The Chevaliers de Ruisse. It was a bluff, that was meant to fool the authorities, but was never meant to harm you."

"But, God forgive us, you were placed in severe danger!"

"It became clear that the plan had been leaked somewhere in the Chevaliers de Ruisse organisation and plans were laid to steal the pearls for other purposes. For a moment he was silent, looking at the grass whilst still clutching her hand. Well, all our plans had gone wrong, for the Chevaliers, and also for the 'free enterprise robbers'."

"Worse than that, you and Anna Romaine had been put in danger, for the real burglars were even more brusque, than would have been the case with a fake robbery! Oh, how I regret not being on duty that morning for I had been assigned to watch with Boris to raise a false alarm over the pearls.

"I now see that from the start, it was a reprehensible plan, but thought that it was foolproof and that it would finance the journey to Switzerland to sell the pearls, then to pay my way in and out of Russia if I was lucky enough to rescue my father."

"The aftershock of the death of Boris did not end there, as soon I was being blackmailed by Georgiou to hand over the pearls to him, by threatening consequences for my father whom I knew to be in a very frail state."

"By this time, I didn't know which way to turn, for I deeply regretted the danger I had put you in. Perhaps this would not have awakened my conscience, I don't know."

"But I had not foreseen that you, my darling, would by now become precious to me and I couldn't anticipate all the consequences of my actions. He was again silent, as he continued to hold her hand fiercely in his. He seemed to withdraw into thoughts for a few minutes and Carole didn't speak, sensing that there were other revelations to come."

"What I didn't then know was that M15 were also interested in me and they offered me a way out in return for my co-operation and I grasped it, thinking that this would help the cause and end the potential danger to you, for I would be long gone and that would be the end of it."

His grip on her hand relaxed slightly and he put it to

the damage part of his face. "But we were both caught in the same net, weren't we? I found that I couldn't forget you, and I hoped that you hadn't forgotten me."

"After the revelations on the quayside, as we left Russia, and after the injury I sustained, I couldn't really think straight. I had brought you back into danger just by being with me, for Georgiou held onto his grudge at losing the pearls, even though he had thought that I had been drowned in the Thames mud along with the pearls."

"Somehow, he saw us together on the Thames and plotted his revenge. I heard that he was looking out for me and thought my disguise would confuse him." By now his voice had dropped to a whisper. "What I didn't anticipate, God forgive me, was that, in his twisted mind, he had planned to use you in such a monstrous display of power to exact his revenge."

"Nicholas, don't take on so." She whispered. "I was stupid."

He looked at her full in the face and she saw such anguish there that she was taken aback.

"But don't you see," He groaned, looking her full in

the face. "It was wrong of me to involve you in such a plot.

In seeking to do something heroic, I DID EVIL and it had EVIL consequences, for I might almost have done the deed myself. I involved you in the plot and I must take responsibility for what happened." His face was ravaged and truly ugly to behold, but his eyes, oh those lovely moonlight eyes, stared at her, half demented by guilt.

She stared back at him, horrified that he had accepted this burden. She turned to him and took his face in her hands. "Don't, don't. It is behind us now." She put her arms around him and cradled his head on her shoulder and he wept.

Sometime later, He led her back out of the lynch gate and along the path to a small grassy corner of a wheat field and drew her to the ground. He stroked her cheek and touched the outline of her nose. She sat, still as a mouse. and with almost the same sense of fear and he held back. He realised that there would be a moment which would be difficult for them both and he didn't know how to proceed.

He took his jumper and made a pillow for them to lie on and he turned on his back looking up at the sky.

The clouds had darkened and the sun was blotted out for longer moments but it was warm and he waited for her to respond. The minutes ticked by whilst she chewed a piece of grass and Nicholas closed his eyes.

Tentatively she put her hand in his. She rolled onto her stomach, and teased him with the grass.

He turned on his side towards her and propped his head in his hand and looked intently at her. She held her eyes downcast until, aware of his steady gaze, she looked back at him. He saw no love in their depths only a blankness that he could not transgress. He looked at her longingly but there was no hunger in her eyes in response.

He rolled over onto his back again, held back from touching her, by the blankness he saw in her eyes. Then drops of rain suddenly fell heavily upon them.

Nicholas jumped up and, grabbing her hand, as they raced back down the hill and arrived breathless in the coppice of trees. He wrapped himself around her to keep her safe from the rain and turned her face to his and kissed her with passion to which she responded with growing passion of her own.

"Caro, Caro, you do want me, you do need me?" He pleaded and she, in an agony of self-abasement, said.

"Nicholas, how could you want me, how could you love me...after...after." Her voice fell away and she hid her face from him. He took her face in his hands and turned her chin up until she was looking into his eyes.

"I do want you, I will always want you. We have both been beaten down one way or another but together we will become stronger. I love you and want us to have a life together. Somehow, I know that we will work it out. We must hold on to the fact that we have both nearly died, because of the savagery of others, but we didn't, and we must be grateful for that and build a meaningful life out of it."

CHAPTER 16

Reconciliation and Home Run

Their lovemaking, when it came, was not a success. Where he had thought to show consideration, the spectre of his enemy came to haunt them, and his manhood failed her.

They had rescued the situation in the morning when they awoke.

He had opened his eyes to find her facing him and he put his hand to her cheek. "I couldn't, I didn't…," he said haltingly. "Did I hurt you." He whispered. She shook her head and pressed her body against him.

"No but I thought you couldn't bear the memory, and I was somehow no longer clean." She said in a muffled voice.

"Well there are many ways to be defiled and we can all feel that about things we have done, and I am certainly not the man that left you here all those months ago; things happen, and sometimes you are not aware how mixed your motives are. I guess I didn't know how I could be tempted by that woman at the Bastille Day, and I felt pretty bad about that display."

"Afterwards I came looking for you to say I was truly sorry that I could be affected by her, but my actions were to blame in chasing you away, so do not take all the blame. Things happen that we cannot always control, but it is how we move on that matters."

"Nicholas, what can we do but accept each other's faults and forgive, oh please, please forgive me." She whispered but he silenced her with a kiss which continued in her ear, and neck and breasts until her nipples hardened and he sucked them with hunger. He traced the line of her navel with kisses until he came to her mount of Venus and there was no hesitation in his mounting as she moaned and twisted under his vigour.

She wrapped her legs around his back and pulled him to her and cried with joy when at last they came, and sank back, his erection slowly receding against her thighs.

****

Later he awoke and all his troubles had washed away. Such a sense of peace had entered his being that he could not begin to contemplate the nightmare he had been living for the past weeks. He decided that they should leave this lovely valley to go to her family home but was reluctant to wake her.

He ordered breakfast and took a shower, all very civilized he realised, as such luxuries had not been part of his routine for many months. He remembered the outside pump at his uncle's farm, and the vigour of cold water. He decided to change the temperature to cold and as he did so he felt arms around him and then a squeal as Carole was doused in the cold water and withdrew.

He chased her round the room and caught up with her again by the shower and this time he held on to her while he adjusted the taps back to warm and pulled her to him. He remembered their shower arrangement in the boat and thought he was now in heaven. Soon they were oblivious to everything but their rising passion and he dimly thought that a full-sized shower head was his next priority wherever he went to live.

****

They had left Berkshire and headed over the Cotswolds to Avonbridge and come to his house next to her family home.

Carole had exclaimed at the innocent deception he had played on her, "Nicholas, how could you, all those weeks you were so near, yet still you didn't speak?"

"I know, and now I feel foolish and untrusting. Forgive me." He said humbly. She looked at him and her heart was full of love. She was fully awakened to the nature of that love and she resolved to cherish him. They had somewhere along the line, moved from bodily passion to a lifetime commitment and no marriage vows were needed, to confirm that for her.

"Before you run off to speak to your parents, let me go next door and invite them to tea. I rather think I would like to meet them on my own territory so to speak, and he embraced her briefly. Carole, in surprise, saw that he was unsure and nervous at the coming introduction and planted a kiss on his nose.

With womanly interest, she inspected the kitchen and looked in the store cupboard. There was tea and sugar to be had but definitely no ingredients for a cake and decided that wouldn't do for afternoon tea. She slipped out of the back door and up the path to 'The Angel,' and through the bar. She saw her friend at the desk, but hurried through into the High Street, to the bakers next door.

With several cakes, fresh bread, bacon and eggs in her arms, she slipped back into the pub and through the back way to the river. She didn't stop to look for her friend, but her friend Margaret saw her and was surprised that Carole was avoiding her. It was so unlike her not to speak, and wondered what was the hurry.

Nicholas was nowhere to be seen and she remembered that he was in her parent's house next door. She busied herself preparing a tray and put the cakes on a dish. She plumped up the cushions and saw the rug ready for use, and wondered why Stefan was not here, in the house? She had not asked Nicholas where his father was. Next, she took her case upstairs and put her nightdress on the bed.

She was very deliberately, telling Nicholas that she

was not going to sleep at her parent's house and there was no going back on her commitment. Such a simple sign but, in their world of coded messages, one he would understand.

Meanwhile Nicholas went to find her parents in the garden and had found them unaware of his arrival.

"Oh hello Mr. Baron. Good to see you again. We thought you had gone away for good when we didn't see you for so long." Said her mother.

"No, no, I have been rather taken up with events in London recently."

"Ah yes, London, such a busy place. It takes over completely. It seems to have swallowed up my daughter." She said peevishly. And Nicholas realised that Carole had not contacted her parents about her trouble. Well, he certainly needed to be careful here, not to say anything.

"Anyway, I am here without my father this time, but I have a guest and thought you might like to come for tea, when you have finished in your garden, about 4.00 p.m. if that suits you?"

"That would be lovely," Said Mr. Semele firmly.

"Oh well, I don't know," Carole's mother said hesitantly.

"Of course, we can." Said her husband with more emphasis. "The garden can wait."

Nicholas looked from one to the other and it was clear to him, that here was a couple who had buried themselves away and had shut the world out.

****

Nicholas had put the chairs in the garden when he heard the doorbell ring. He ushered them through the French windows and onto a small terrace above the river. They sat down and exclaimed at the growth of the bushes.

"Your lovely rose bush has seen better moments. I see you have had little time to cut back your dead blooms."

"No." Said Nicholas. "I had envisaged my father would spend more time here this summer, but circumstances have meant, that he has been staying with friends."

"Such a pity." Said Carole's mother. "We rather looked forward to having a neighbour again. Are you planning to come down more often?"

"Well yes, I hope so." He said diffidently, "Ah, here comes the tea. Allow me to introduce you, or perhaps no introduction is needed, to my wife to be, I hope." And he looked challengingly at Carole who smiled back at him, blushing.

"What, Carole? What is this? Where have you sprung from?" But there could be nothing ambiguous about the way Nicholas took her hand and kissed it.

"How? Where? What is this? We have been worried about you." And both her parents hugged Carole to them.

"Did I hear right? That this is your fiancé?"

"I think that is so." She said directly to Nicholas and he gazed back with a lopsided grin on his damaged face.

"Now." She said. This tea is getting cold. Would you like milk or lemon?" And the questions kept coming as they all adjusted to the new reality and drank their tea.

The next morning, they rose early and answered the call of the bells.

Nicholas knelt down in a pew looking up at the wonderful vaulted ceiling above.

He had heard on the radio that morning the whole sorry story of the politician and the call girls as it burst upon the nation. So sordid. Such a waste of a man's talents, who had been destroyed by his passions.

Nicholas felt no sense of triumph at his part in the investigation, especially when he had been so involved in the personal tragedy that had followed.

He wondered how many others would be broken by the revelations and he thought of Georgiou. He had tried desperately to avoid thinking of the man, who was indeed his enemy. He had acknowledged that now, for he knew him for a malicious sadist. But would he ever be brought to justice? Someday, there must be a reckoning, he vowed.

He had evaded the law once before and Nicholas now saw that he would evade it again. 'Sending him to Siberia,' would be too good for his likes. Nicholas hoped that one day, he would be returned to Russia to be dealt with.

Georgiou's father had evoked diplomatic immunity again, through his position in the Embassy, so there was nothing they could do to bring him to justice this time.

Georgiou's treatment of Carole had been gross in the extreme and had almost broken her, but he had not, and Nicholas thanked God for it. He began to think of his own actions during the past year and wished to be done with this underworld of deceit. It crept into the very fibre of his being, he thought. For nine months, he had lived with deceit during his travels and he was ashamed, just how easily lies, tripped off his tongue.

He had thought that rescuing his father from Siberia would be a noble thing, but he had learnt to lie and deceive with great ease.

He thought of their night of passion and fervently longed to be whole again. But the cloak of deception waited to claim him again and he knew it.

All he could hope for, was to examine his reasons for doing his master's bidding.

Somehow, he had to build a better place in the world, and he began to think of how he could make a difference for others. He had led a self-centered life so far, and had enjoyed all the fruits of an English education.

His time, travelling Europe, had been a test of

endurance and resolve, and it had hardened those qualities in him, but now knew, he must use those to make a better world. They had both been scarred by their involvement in spying but together they could build something positive, couldn't they?

AUTHORS NOTES

There was an infamous true story at about the time I have set this novel, of a woman bringing down the Minister for War over a possible breach in security, and my plot is very loosely based on this 'cause celebre'. I have woven the facts to suit my story but there were many more twists and turns before her sad tale was over.

Note: I have given Nicholas' cruiser the extra dimension of having been one of the little boats that took part in rescuing soldiers from the beaches of Picardy. This was after the unsuccessful expeditionary forces' hasty retreat in the face of annihilation, at the beginning of WW2.

They came from all the river estuaries around London and the south coast of England and many of these veterans may still occasionally be spotted on the lower reaches of the Thames, where they have been lovingly cared for.

ACKNOWLEDGEMENTS

To Vivienne and PaTrisha-Anne for continuing to be my support, and all my scattered family worldwide, for enthusiastically spreading the word of my stories on their home patch.

I would also like to give my special thanks to Olivia, for her artistic talents of make-up, hair styling and taking my photograph – a miracle of technology!

If you have enjoyed this book, there are other books in the series for you to read,

BOOK 1

THE PRISONER AND THE PEARLS

Nicholas Baron, abandoned orphan from war-torn Europe, is destined to return to Russia. He is recruited by the Chevaliers de Russie to attempt to rescue a dissident author from Siberia.

But the plan is not as simple as it seems. First there is an unexplained death which threatens the life of an innocent young woman.

Danger and deceit, love and liberty, entwine in this world of spies and double dealing, in this first book of the series.

SEA SPRITE AND SUBMARINES Autumn1962
North Atlantic

Russian submarines, with cargoes bound for Cuba, are on a collision course with the USS Navy fleet.

After a family celebration, Nicholas Baron and Carole Semele are recalled to Whitehall. Sir Charles Willingham Wright Section Head. M15, must put together a crack team to help avert confrontation between the two nations. to give them time to come to their senses.

But must this also be at personal cost to the young lovers, who are caught up in a dual with an old adversary which leaves two people dead?

The world watches events as the submarines move closer, but who will blink first?

MEL FLAVELL

November 2017

www.ingramcontent.com/pod-product-compliance
Lightning Source LLC
Chambersburg PA
CBHW062124170626
46813CB00002B/562